A Pinch of Coriander

Available Now

A Pinch of Coriander:
Book One
Time Will Tell

A Pinch of Coriander:
Book Two
The Truth About Secrets

A Pinch of Coriander:
Book Three
Long Way Home

A Pinch of Coriander

Book Three:
Long Way Home

Loretta Gatto-White

Loretta Gatto-White, Publisher: https://gattowhitewrites.com

Cover designed by Kate Cowan

ISBN 978-1-7750341-4-8 (Paperback edition)
ISBN 978-1-7750341-5-5 (eBook edition)

Print Edition

Chapter One

SPRING

NICK WAS HOME from Oxford, resolute in his beliefs and having made his peace, outwardly at least, about Lidia's fidelity and Frank's perfidy. For the next two weeks, relations slowly warmed between Nick and Lidia. Nick became more communicative, and affectionate, if not passionate. That was a relief, a reassurance, as Lidia had, with apprehension, intuited the anger brewing in her husband since Frank left. And, although Nick's planning to see him in Oxford worried her, she felt sure Frank would protect her.

If nothing else, at the very least, his being a priest, made Frank Kelley very good at keeping secrets. None the less, during February, she tried to write several emails to him, but always discarded instead of sending, perhaps it was just 'talking' with herself that she needed, more than communicating with Frank? In any case, he had made no attempt to contact her, keeping their tacit agreement.

So, Lidia put him out of her mind, and focussed instead on Antonio, who was becoming more precocious by the day, and on the needs of her friends, especially Paul and Ramona, whom she invited for dinner.

They were both understandably subdued but resigned to the advice that they should not try for a child again. Nick and Paul had a moment together in the garden, where Nick felt an inexplicable unease, like guilt, as he bounced Antonio on his knee, and listened to Paul's revelation of regret at not being able to have a child with Ramona. He'd never seen this tender side of Paul before, added to the fact that he'd already fathered three children, it surprised Nick that he mourned so deeply for this loss.

Unhappy that he could do no more for his grieving friend but listen and sympathize, Nick, felt himself more than ever, counting his blessing in the unexpected, delightful gift of Antonio.

LIDIA'S DOMESTIC LIFE continued without drama, freeing her mind to concentrate on her blog and summer features, 'Cottaging: Best Guest Rules,' and

'Not in My Backyard! Your Pool, Your Privacy', issues that she gathered from her social media exchanges, needed addressing.

In addition, she had worked hard on research for the fall edition, keeping her editorial hand-in, preparing for her return to work. So, it was with confidence that Lidia took her seat early in the magazine's board room, sipping her chai latte, looking over her notes, waiting for Brunhilde and her editorial entourage to emerge.

She checked the time, it was now ten minutes past their appointment, and not like Brunhilde to be late. Lidia worried she'd got the date or time wrong and was checking her calendar when Shelton joined her.

"Ah! Miss Mew, long time, no see. You look glorious," he exclaimed, sitting next to her, appraising his friend's new outfit.

"Thanks Shelton, I bought it specially for the meeting. I wanted to look fresh and raring to get back to work," she said with a big grin.

"Well Miss Mew, that pale blue linen sheath does the trick. And the beautiful orange silk scarf, with all the lovely butterflies. Just the right touch, very springy."

"I love it too, it was Lo's, a memento I kept of her."

"Speaking of keeping things, our Brunhilde seems uncharacteristically bad at time-keeping today. Where is everybody anyway?" he asked, turning to look-out the glass wall, "I hope this starts soon, I've an egregious vodka-cooler launch at five," he said, impatiently checking his emails.

Just then, Siobhan entered, took a seat at the head of the conference table, greeted them both and apologized for the late start. Opening her first folder, she began by addressing Lidia, when Shelton, cut her off, "Is this it? No offence, Siobhan, but I was under the impression that it was all hands-on deck to this meeting, chaired by our Editor-In-Chief."

Siobhan looked a little nervous, cleared her throat, and said, "Sorry Shelton, if the memo gave you that impression, but actually, it's just you and Lidia that Ms. Braun wanted me to see."

"Hmm, why do I sense an ambush?" Shelton said, swivelling a little to address Lidia.

"Oh, don't be so paranoid, Shelton. I'm sure our trusted colleague here, has a good reason for wanting to deal with us alone. It's more efficient, right Siobhan?" Lidia smiled reassuringly.

Siobhan smiled weakly at Lidia, and said, "Well, it's more privacy that's the issue. You see Lidia, it's been decided that your summer columns will be the last of 'Manners Matter'. It appears that manners don't really matter that much to our readers, not the demographic we're currently after anyway."

"Oh," Lidia said taken aback, "well, then… Um, what about this, I could pen a column on the trials, tribulations and joys of mid-life motherhood?" she said her voice rising, grasping at straws for inspiration.

"I'm afraid not. The new demo we need to reach is late millennials, you know, the 'Yummy Mummy's', like our staff in 'What We Love Now' and well, me, I guess," she said, with a curt smile, and a little shrug.

Shelton literally twiddled his thumbs and observed the exchange with interest and more than a little apprehension.

"Well then, what content do you, I mean Ms. Braun, foresee me contributing when I return as editor?"

Sighing deeply, she took an envelope from her file, looked down somberly and said, "Lidia, you and I have been friends for ages, and I want you to know it causes me a great deal of pain to tell you that Ms. Braun has offered me the editorial position permanently. So, although your contributions to the success of this magazine are appreciated, and will not go unacknowledged, they are no longer necessary, freeing you to explore other horizons for your awesome creativity and spend more precious time with your growing child."

She placed the envelope in front of an astounded Lidia, who turned-on her and shouted, "You ageist bitch! Yummy Mummy's are in and perimenopausal ones out, is that it? No longer useful, because of our age?"

"Your words, not mine," Siobhan countered, mindful of avoiding any labor tribunal revenge.

"Your thoughts, Siobhan!"

"Oh, so now you're clairvoyant?"

"Yeah, that's right, cause I can see right through you, *friend*!"

Siobhan relaxed her jaw, composed herself, and in a calm, even voice, said, "I know you are understandably upset, so perhaps you should go now. We'll talk together later about this issue, just you and me, okay?"

"No way, I'm staying here. Just in case Shelton needs a witness to his brutal axing too. I suppose being willing to wield Brunilda's battle-ax is the price you paid to usurp me."

"Well, Siobhan? C'mon, let's get this over with. What about me?" Shelton looked at her hard.

"You're in the same position. Look, this isn't my doing, but Brunilda wants me to just do the drinks pairings as part of my food column. No more sniffing, swishing and spitting-out, or obtuse, improbable, elitist tasting notes a paragraph long!" Siobhan said, flushed and exasperated.

"So, more room for ad copy, no more room for Shelton. Payroll cut, revenue enhanced, I get it."

"For what it's worth, you two, I agree with Brunhilde. Without these changes, amongst others, and a failure to capture new readership, we're sunk. And I, like you, have a family to feed too. So yes, I'm sorry to be doing this, but it must be done!" she declared, slapping her palm on the table. Then sliding Shelton his envelope, she rose abruptly, and left the room.

Lidia looked at Shelton, worried, "What are we going to do?"

"Do you have your press pass?"

"Yes, why?"

"Because we're going to Sunnyside to crash this hip-hop, vodka cooler bash, get drunk and behave badly. Will that do for now, Miss Mew?"

"Yes, Shelton. I think that'll do."

LIDIA AND SHELTON took a breezy cab ride along Lakeshore Boulevard to Sunnyside, a once splendid,

1920's Beaux Arts complex of dance halls, bandstand, amusement park, restaurants and bathing pavilions on the city's north shore of Lake Ontario. The roaring twenties, nineteen-million-dollar triumph of cutting-edge aesthetic municipal infrastructure for the pure entertainment of its hoi polloi, was now reduced to the mere façade of the beautiful bathing pavilion, a dance hall, and a restaurant complex. The rest, being plowed under for the transverse that is the Gardiner Expressway, an elevated eyesore, followed by a blight of condominiums, which cut-off the city from its shoreline, its populace from the recreation of the lake.

After flashing their press cards past the security thugs, Lidia and Shelton were assaulted by the rapper's image fronting the brand, sneering down at them from a series of big screens, while lithe young women in various stages of undress, writhed and wriggled all over and around him. The loud, thumping bass backed his chorus of "Booty-Boom, Booty-Boom, Booty Boom, Boom, Boom," in what seemed an eternal loop.

Strobes flashed as servers in tiny metallic shorts and sequined bras bopped around the room carrying trays of snacks. Shelton and Lidia were wolfing down a couple of chicken nuggets, when a dancer slid-up to Shelton and began to twerk, "Oh save it girl, you're firing that-off in the wrong direction," Shelton said in his campiest voice.

Lidia laughed, then grabbed a cone of curly fries with chipotle mayo, offering some to Shelton, she said, "Hmm, who do you think's catering this shindig?"

"By the quality of the comestibles, I'd say The Colonel."

They both snickered at this when a tray of popcorn shrimp sailed by. After sampling some of them, Shelton suggested they make their way over to the colorful display of coolers. They sampled several, throwing back each shot quickly, trying not to taste the cloying flavors.

When the crowd and the music got too annoying, Shelton suggested to Lidia, "You go grab a couple bags of that caramel corn, I'll snatch a few coolers", he said, sliding two into his pockets, then grabbing one in each hand, "and we'll head to the beach, okay?"

"Sounds good, I need some fresh air and quiet," she agreed, massaging her temples.

They slipped-out a side door, past a clutch of smokers, out to the boardwalk and onto the sand, where they parked themselves on two colorful Muskoka chairs near the water's edge. They kicked-off their shoes, Shelton handed Lidia a cooler, relieving her of a bag of salted caramel corn in the process.

She put her head back for a moment, closed her eyes and sighed, "Ah, that's better. Now, what flavor do we have here, I wonder," opening the cooler and sniffing, "Yuck, coconut. What's yours Shelton?"

"Um, peach-mango. Quite the distillation triumph these, eh? Alcoholic suntan lotion and fruity shampoo. Oh well, down the hatch!" he took a deep swig, Lidia followed, sputtering most of hers out.

"God these really are the worst shit, aren't they? Have some popcorn to soak-up the taste," Lidia said, popping a cluster in her mouth.

"Mine's not too bad, let's switch," Shelton offered.

"Okay, if you don't mind coconut," Lidia passed her bottle.

"I do enjoy a pina colada, when in the tropics."

"Well, it's warmish, the sun's out and we're on a beach," Lidia said, getting ready to sample the peach-mango.

"Close enough! Here goes," Shelton took a hearty swig, then grimacing, wiped his mouth.

"Ha! Told ya," Lidia laughed eating more popcorn.

"I'm too nice, that's my problem. Too much the proper gentleman, an anachronism nowadays," he sighed, becoming melancholy. "I blame my mother."

"Oh, doesn't everyone," Lidia said, feeling morose herself.

"No, I mean it. She tried her best, but overcompensated for being poor. Raising me to have Victorian manners, and good speech cost her nothing, hoping they would open doors for me she couldn't afford to open otherwise."

"Where *did* you grow-up, Shelton?"

"In the tiny fishing village of Blue Rocks, Nova Scotia, on the wrong side o' the tracks of Lunenburg."

"Really? I never would've guessed, except that you did seem to know your way around Nova Scotia really well when we were there."

"I wasn't sure you'd noticed. Anyway, as I said, I'm from a small fishing village, the son of a son, of a son, of a scallop man. The guys that go out on the big trawlers in the Bay of Fundy, raking-up it's bottom and breaking their backs to bring you the precious scallop… can't stand them myself.

"Tradition in Blue Rocks is, when you're thirteen, you go to sea with your 'old feller'. Only mine was lost at sea when I was ten…so I was spared that experience. Luckily, I had a spinster aunt, who was a teacher in Lunenburg, she took me in, so I could attend the Lunenburg Academy, and continue in secondary education."

"So, how was it growing-up gay in Blue Rocks? Were you ostracized?" Lidia asked.

"What? No, I'd never come-out in Blue Rocks, there was no gay pride there, Lidia, only gay shame," Shelton chortled, opening another cooler. "Anyway, my ludicrously formal diction was bad enough."

"When did you come out?"

"When I did what most Maritimers do, 'went down the road'. I headed for 'the big smoke' with two Brook's Brothers suits, an overcoat, and two silk ties, all of which I paid the princely sum of twenty-five bucks for at 'Frenchies', our iconic used clothing emporium.

"I got an apprenticeship at one of Toronto's best be-spoke clothiers, it paid shit, the prestige, supposing to compensate. So, me and the other apprentices did it for the prestige. We also did it for dinner, blowing the old moneybags for a posh nosh at La Scala, Hy's or Three Small Rooms. Once I even got into The Brazilian Ball, back then, the social event of the year.

"Some did it for apartments too. But all I wanted was to eat the gourmet food, drink the fine wine, experience it, learn about it. Move and groove in the social sphere of the rich, and save enough money to take the sommelier course, then I'd be made," he said, slurring his words a little.

"And you did make it, Shelton. You're a success!" Lidia exclaimed, taking another drink.

"Yeah, except now, I'm like my old feller, lost at sea, no longer wanted on the voyage!" Shelton shouted, trying to stand, swaying.

Lidia stood too, and just as she was about to suggest calling it a day and getting a cab home, the wind picked-up, carrying her scarf out to the water, where it floated in, then away from the shore. Looking sadly after it, "Oh my pretty scarf, Lo's scarf," she moaned tipsily.

"Don't worry, Miss Mew, it's Shelton to the rescue!" he yelled, pulling off his trousers, tossing aside his jacket, and marching resolutely into the water.

Lidia wobbled after him, "No Shelton! You big idiot! Come back, you'll get all wet."

He was in up to his knees, when he grabbed the scarf on the waves as they rushed in. Then he turned to shore, grinning, waving it above his head like a banner, when a big roller came crashing down, flattening him on the beach. Lidia ran over, struggling to get him to his feet, when a police boat, bearing two officers, stopped-by. One of them shouted from an intercom, "Hey, is he alright?"

"Yes, oh yes officer. He just wanted to get my scarf…it's a special scarf, see," she held-up the limp, sodden mess as proof.

"Have you two been drinking?" the officer asked.

"Oh no," she answered, shaking her head emphatically, then looking down at her companion, "Well, he has, just a little. I'm going get his pants on, then get him in a cab, okay?"

"See that you do and stay out of the water. Got it?"

"Oh yes, officer. Got it!" she said, giving him a thumbs-up.

The engine revved, and they sped-off towards a rowdy crowd, beyond the board walk, playing Frisbee in the water.

Lidia got Shelton back to his chair, "Now, sit down, and slip-off those boxers."

"Oh, Miss Mew! I do declare, you are a brazen hussy," Shelton said laughing, batting his eyelashes at her.

"Shut-up Shelton, and just do it!"

He struggled for a few seconds. Then, exasperated, shot up and pulled them off. Lidia tried to cover his crotch with the wet scarf, only to have Shelton jiggle at her.

"Just sit down, you fool, and leave that scarf there, while I get your pants on. If those cops come back, we're in trouble," she said angrily, pulling-up her dress, kneeling in the sand, she peeled-off his wet socks, then tried to get his feet into each trouser leg and up to his thighs.

"Why? No trouble, Mew. There were two of them, and I call dibs on the tanned blonde," he said between hiccups and giggles.

"Right," Lidia stood, brushing the sand from her knees, ignoring his silliness. "Now Shelton, you've got to stand quickly, and on the count of three, pull those trousers up. Got it?"

"Got it! Mein Herr," he said, saluting.

Lidia grabbed his forearms, "One, two, three!"

Shelton jumped-up, and his trousers fell down, "Oops!"

"Oh shit, Shelton!" Lidia slapped her arms against her thighs, grabbed her purse and scarf, and stomped away fuming.

Shelton shrugged, bent over, pulled-up his trousers, grabbed his underwear and shoes and followed, past the onlooking group of smokers, who snickered and cat-called. He looked-over his shoulder, blew an air kiss, tossing his wet socks and pants at them.

DISGRACE

LIDIA CLIMBED THE stairs to the bedroom, seeing the

night-light from the landing, she tread softly, and stood at the foot of the bed, damp and dishevelled. Antonio was snoozing loudly, cradled into Nick, who, perceiving her presence, awoke abruptly, raising himself on one elbow, squinting to focus his eyes.

He whispered at her angrily, "Where've you been? I called the office and Siobhan, everyone's gone to voice mail, including you. How dare you worry me like this. And what the hell have you been doing? You reek!"

Lidia answered in a weak, pitiable voice, "I was sacked. Shelton and I were sacked, no warning, nothing. So, we went out together to a party, at Sunnyside and…"

"You know what? I don't want to hear it, you're a disgrace. Go sleep downstairs," he said as he punched his pillow, laid back down, and feigned sleep.

"I'm sorry, Nick…I'm so sorry for everything," she pleaded quietly, then went to make her bed in the den, too tired and cold sober now, to even cry.

The next morning, the aroma of freshly-brewed coffee brought Lidia to her senses, as Nick placed a cappuccino at her bedside and gently shook her shoulder, "Hey you, wake-up. I have to go in an hour, and you need to look after Antonio."

"Ugh, okay, okay. Be there in a minute. Is there any Tylenol?"

"It's on the saucer and here's your robe," Nick replied, tossing it on the bed, then leaving her to get herself together.

When she emerged into the kitchen, Antonio was in his highchair, making a mucky mess of a few slices of banana. He looked-up at her, holding his mushy offering and shouted, "Ma! Ma!" smacking his lips. She bent down and gave him a kiss, miming eating the fruit he held-up, making funny faces, which made him giggle.

She plopped down in the chair beside him, not daring to venture a kiss from Nick, who was at the stove, making them scrambled eggs. As he set hers down in front of her, she said contritely, "Nick, I'm so sorry, I acted like a selfish –

"I know," Nick cut her-off, "like a selfish idiot. So, please spare me a post-mortem of your shame, and address the important issue. The issue of your being unemployed, sabotaging my paternity leave," he said coldly, buttering his toast.

"Again, I'm sorry. I had no idea this was coming, neither did Shelton. Clive had no clue either. Brunhilde and Siobhan kept this very much on the downlow. I don't know what to say, except we have to crunch some numbers, figure out a way to balance the budget until I get work."

"First, we have to rent that empty basement apartment, I'm going to ask around at the college."

"But, what about Jesse?"

"She can buy a futon, shack-up in the loft with her little brother, and start paying her way," Nick said resolutely.

"Now, you sound like me," Lidia chuckled, then seeing her husband's poker-face, went on, "couldn't you postpone your leave?"

"No, I couldn't, it's all arranged to begin in September. Look, I didn't get to spend much time with Jess when she was an infant, but I can with Antonio, and I'm going to," Nick declared, getting-up, taking his plate to the dishwasher.

"Okay, good. If that's what you want love, we'll find a way to make it happen," she said, giving him a little smile. "And leave those things, I'll clean-up, you've got to go."

"Finish your eggs, they're getting cold…you need something in your stomach," he replied, putting on his jacket, heading for the front door, stopping to give Antonio a kiss. He hesitated, then turned to give Lidia one too.

After she got herself together and took Antonio out for his walk, Lidia slowly formulated a plan. A new approach to their dilemma, for which she needed to do some research.

While her son napped, she created a spreadsheet of their current fixed expenditures, then Nick's income, her severance pay, unemployment benefits, potential rent for the basement apartment and assets.

Then she did research on long-term apartment rentals in the fall in Tuscany, average cost of living in each desirable location, and cost of extended health care. After tallying all the columns and balancing them, she found with glee, that they could do it!

She could hardly wait until Nick got home to give him the news, this was her offering, to balance their lives and mend their marriage. She desperately needed to give him this, he would be so happy.

When Nick got home, he found Lidia and Antonio in the kitchen, joining them, he pulled Antonio up on his knee, where he sucked away happily on the end of his father's tie.

"What's all this?" Nick asked wearily, looking over Lidia's spread sheet and printouts. "Tuscan rentals? We can't afford a vacation."

"It's not a vacation, it's a 'time out'. And yes, we can afford it. Quite easily, actually. I tallied all our expenditures here, where we can cut back, like not renewing the lease on the car, and eating out. And this column is income from the basement, unemployment and leave benefits, my retirement savings withdrawal and line of credit –"

"Whoa, what 'line of credit', and 'No!', to withdrawing from your RRSP."

Lidia sighed, "'Yes', to the withdrawal, as I'll make it when my benefit runs out, so I won't be dinged with tons of tax, and the line of credit we can get for a bargain, secured on our other investments. Look, this is the maximum the bank will lend, and it's for an emergency fund, we may not even use it. But it's good to have when living abroad."

"Living abroad? In Tuscany? And for how long?" Nick asked warily.

"For six months, September to January, in any of these five cities in Tuscany. Here, take a look. These are the monthly rates, locations, and amenities. My preference is Florence or Siena…but it's whatever you want. All of the apartments are in the city centre, we won't even need a car!" Lidia said, pleased with herself.

"Hmm," Nick said as he handed Antonio to Lidia, and pored-over the spread sheet and printouts. Lidia looked-on with anticipation, her eyes pleading, *please, say yes!*

Then, straightening his back and leaning against the chair, he looked thoughtful and said, "Christmas in Florence. That's what I vote for. Let it be Florence," he decided.

"Yay! That's what I hoped you'd say! Remember Nick? Florence is special to us."

"Oh yes, I remember. We courted in Rome for a month and fornicated in Florence for a week, didn't see the Accademia, the Uffizi or the Bargello...but we sure saw a lot of each other," he said with a grin.

Lidia giggled, covering her son's ears, blushing a little at the memory.

"Okay, this calls for a toast with a good Chianti. Let's see what I've got in the wine rack." He left whistling, '*Le donne e mobile*' and returned bearing a dusty bottle, a 2008 Chianti Classico riserva.

"Salute, amore!" Lidia said, raising her glass to her husband. "My God, Nick, we have to brush-up on our Italian, we haven't spoken it in years."

"Well, we have a few months, we should start talking a little to Antonio too. Jesse's Italian's pretty spotty, I wished she'd applied herself more in Heritage Language classes," he sighed, taking a sip of wine.

"Her Italian's not so bad, she can hold a basic conversation. Anyway, back to our plans. I'll still circulate my c.v., but I don't think I'll get any joy there, magazine publishing being what it is, at the moment. I can get freelance work, especially doing features on Tuscany from abroad. Doesn't pay very much anymore, but it'll keep us in wine, and 'little man' here, in diapers. And you Nick, you can start getting material for that cookbook, plot-out your novel too," Lidia said with enthusiasm.

"Yes, I could, couldn't, I?"

"Oh, and a blog, Nick, you should start a blog. I can help you get started, it's easy. Call it 'Time-out in Tuscany'."

"Or, 'A Pinch of Coriander'; 'Time-out in Tuscany' won't work when we come back," Nick advised, pouring himself another glass, handing Antonio's juice bottle to Lidia.

"That's if we ever come back," Lidia laughed.

HELLO, GOODBYE

MARCH BREAK WAS over, and a hungry, jet-lagged Lucinda had just returned home. She put-in a week's load of laundry and was whipping-up an omelet, when her father dropped-in on his way to an appointment.

"Hey sweetheart, how are you? How was the trip?" he asked, entering the kitchen area to greet his daughter with a hug and a kiss.

"It was good, dad. I'm just a little tired and *really* hungry," she said hugging him back. "This cheese and chive omelet's big enough for two, want some?"

"Okay, but just a little, I have to go soon," he replied, reaching up for two plates, then getting-out the knives and forks. "How's Valentina? You two got along okay?"

"Oh, mom's much better, getting over Hans, being busy helps. And yes, we got along really well. I'm glad we reconnected, just the two of us this time, it made a difference, dad. I guess it's also because she sees I'm responsible now, that she treats me more like an adult."

"That's good, I'm glad." As they ate their lunch, Javi observed, "Well, I guess it's back to the grind-stone for you tomorrow, no more sunning and sleeping-in."

"Actually, I did neither while I was away, too busy helping-out in the winery."

"Yeah, you're barely tanned. Why were you help-ing out? Were they short-staffed?'

"No, although the tasting-room was really busy. Oh, and before I forget, I brought back some of our 1997 Malbec, my birthday vintage," Lucinda said, taking their empty plates to the dishwasher. "I liked working there, dad. I'm interested in the business, and it was fun.

"In fact, I got-up with the sun every morning, and with Uncle Hector, on horseback, toured the vines. It was magic, dad, the quiet of the early morning, the freshness of the mountain air…the mist burning-off in the rising sun. I forgot how beautiful our land was," Lucinda said, suddenly standing very still, her eyes lit-up, as if in that place, experiencing the moment again.

"Oh yes, I remember. I loved it too, wanted to make my home there, but it wasn't to be," Javi sighed, rising.

"I know dad, but that's in your past…. um, can you stay for a few minutes longer? I need to tell you something," Lucinda said, sitting back down at the table.

Javi consented, "Sure, I have a little time – shoot."

"You know Mendoza, the family, the winery, it's in your past…right?" Lucinda nodded at her father.

"Yes, it is, except for you. Through you, I'll always have a connection to Mendoza and Valentina," Javi said, slightly puzzled.

"But it's not the past for me, it's my future dad, not Toronto, not school. The winery, the family, the legacy you left me, our land. That's my future," Lucinda said, passionately.

Javi looked down and thought a moment, "I see, so not school, not here, and I guess not with me. Is that right?" he asked looking-up, with sad eyes.

"Dad, no! You'll always be –

"Yeah, yeah, I know, 'my dad'. Can't deny it, as you said, it's a matter of record," he replied flatly, pushing his chair back, getting-up to go.

"Dad, please!" Lucinda grabbed his lapel, "I love you, you saved me from being a lonely little girl. But I've grown-up now. Because of you, I've come up well, I think," she laughed, tears in her eyes.

Softening, Javi said, "We've grown-up together Lucinda, and yes, we've grown-up well."

They both sat down again and looked at each other for a few moments in silence. Javi tightened his lips, raised an eyebrow, and fixed Lucinda with a sharp stare. Lucinda met his eyes dead-on and stared right back. Her shoulders began to tremble, as she tried to suppress a titter, then they both broke-out in fits of laughter.

"Will you come back? To walk me down the aisle?" Javi managed to blurt out.

"Oh yes, but only if I get to wear a tux," Lucinda said.

"Sure, lavender, with sequined lapels, the full Liberace, if that's what it takes," Javi laughed some more.

"That's what it takes, but you have to wear the same one too!" Lucinda said, starting the laughter at the thought of them at the altar, in twin lavender tuxedos.

They both wiped their eyes and calmed down, when Javi asked, "When will you go?"

"First of April."

"So, we have some time then," he said, with a smile.

"Yes, we have some time."

"And what about the love of your life?" Javi asked.

"What? Who do you mean?" Lucinda asked warily.

"Frida, of course."

"Oh, I planned to go riding tomorrow, can't wait to see her. She's the best, and now, most calm, sweet-natured being, good listener too. She was my therapy. When you gave her to me, I felt so much better. I finally felt at home."

"Then you should consider donating her as a therapy horse. There are foundations that need good-natured, healthy horses for people with physical and mental challenges."

"That's a great idea, dad."

"Okay, you do the research on the one's here in Ontario, then we'll plan from there. Let that be your project before you leave… Speaking of leaving, I'd better get a move on," he said, checking his watch.

Lucinda kissed him goodbye, then cleaned-up the cooking mess. After everything was nice and tidy, she quietly stood behind the gleaming kitchen counter, looking out on to the sunlit living-dining area, and the cozy family space, she pictured she and Javi, wolfing-down his super-choris, laughing out loud at 'Raised by Wolves'; just the healing balm she needed for her wounded spirit. She could see the lights and hear the music and laughter of her first Christmas in this home… her abue's nativity all lit-up in pride of place, the perfect tree, the perfect party, she was so happy then.

But that was then. Now, she had to do the business of tidying-up the loose ends of her life, and move-on, leaving the pain, taking only the joy.

IT'S RAINING, IT'S POURING

APRIL ARRIVED TOO quickly for Javi, who had felt a bit side-lined by all of Lucinda's friends wanting to take her out and spend time with her before she left for Argentina. He hadn't quite appreciated how well-liked and popular his beautiful daughter had become. In consolation, they made a pact that she would spend every Christmas with him in Toronto, but he feared that was a promise meant, in time, to be broken.

Now, after he'd just driven a tense hour, often hydroplaning in the pounding spring rain, to see his daughter off at the airport, on the next chapter of her life; the return to her home in Mendoza, it still seemed too soon.

"Are you sure you don't want me to wait with you? You've got plenty of time before you need to check-in at Departures," Javi said nervously, shouldering her carry-on.

"No dad, really, I'm alright. I'd prefer to get in early and just chill, thanks anyway," she said, taking her bag from him.

"Okay, I guess you'll be comfortable in the business class lounge, just don't try to get any drinks. It's a long flight and I don't want you sozzled when you get there," Javi warned.

"I won't, dad. And thanks for up-grading my ticket."

"Yeah well, just remember that's all your birthday and Christmas presents for the next decade," Javi laughed.

Lucinda reached-up to him for a kiss and a hug, before saying their goodbyes. Javi watched as she paused beneath the entrance sign for the lounge, turning to smile and wave at him one last time.

Javi made his way to the car, his umbrella and most of his back dripping wet from the punishing rain. Sitting in the driver's seat, he exhaled deeply, hugged the steering wheel, rested his head on his arms, and wept. Recalling the first time he held her in the delivery room, he wept then, but didn't understand why. Now, he understood.

Chapter Two

CHRISTOS ANESTI

WINTER IN CORFU, the Emerald Isle of Greece, the second largest Greek island next to Crete, is a cool, wet affair. A season made for brooding on the caprices of cruel fate, and Aldo felt in his bones, grief was taking the opportunity to overtake him.

He'd experienced loss and tragedy before in his personal life, witnessed it as a young boy growing-up in an Italy recovering from the horrors of the Second World War. But this grief was different. He came to understand that it was his duty, not to grieve the loss of his charming friend, Lola, but to mourn for the loss of her future as she would've, a kind of grief-by-proxy. He had to do it for her, what she couldn't do for herself.

So, he withdrew, and contemplated, pondering and brooding on how he should honor his friend, sometimes taking long mountain walks in the spitting rain, at others, immersed in the dreariness of the cold, grey sea. As he walked, he talked to her, comforting her, feeling her just one light step, one cool breath, beside him. He didn't want Lola to miss this world, it was a tragic comedy anyway. He wanted her to move on while 'becoming', was still asleep. He didn't want her to see the sun, she'd be too sad, if she did.

But inevitably, spring did arrive with abundant sunlight, bursting all the rosy buds on the Judas trees, blanketing the mountainsides and meadows with a flush of showy, fragrant wildflowers, exciting the buzzing bees. Suddenly, his grief vanished, to where, he did not know. Perhaps it was carried away on the warm breezes, heavy with the herbaceous scent of the leafing olive, the spicy balm of cypress, and the sweetly fragrant kumquat.

The grieving time was over. All the splendor that slept in winter's keep emerged, pushing back the dark and the cold, giving rise to illumination; it was spring in Corfu, and Aldo was inspired.

AS JESSE APPROACHED the restaurant kitchen, she could hear her grandfather whistling as he worked, that was always a good sign, she and Voula were relieved now he seemed to be his old industrious self.

"You rang, master?" Jesse said, looking over Aldo's shoulder.

He put down his mezzaluna and turned to face her, "Yes, pussycat, I have a job for you," he said, smiling his best 'salesman smile'.

"Oh no! It better not be to peel and chop that basket of shallots. Nonno, you know it makes my eyes swell-up just looking at them. Can't I peel spuds, or carrots or something? Please, anything but those damn shallots!" she said, backing away.

"Relax, it's not your knife skills I'm interested in, clumsy as they are. This is an artistic commission. Sit, and I'll tell you about it," he said, pushing a stool her way.

Jesse listened attentively as Aldo explained his plan, "I want to commemorate Lo, she loved Corfu and dreamed of buying a little stone cottage in the mountains, a kind of retreat for her and her friends to come and write and sing, and just hang-out. So, I wanted a memorial to her here. Also, this is where we first met."

"And you thought what exactly? This is a restaurant, not a cenotaph, nonno."

"I thought," Aldo said, raising his hand against any further objections, "about the bar, I'm going to name it, The Lola Lounge, and I want a nice big picture of her above that bar…bold and colorful. And no offence, Jess, but no collage. I want a real painting, okay?"

"Yeah, I figured. I can do what you want in acrylic, how big is big?"

"Oh, I dunno," Aldo squinted and opened his arms wide, "about this big."

"I think I can order a pre-stretched canvas in town, maybe as big as four by six? I'd have to ask them though, but I'm pretty sure it's doable. Any other details to share?"

"Yeah, I want her sat, like a queen, on a red velvet chaise, in a garden, outside a stone cottage, surrounded by flowers, with a King Charles Cavalier spaniel…white and tan, do you know that breed?"

"Yes, I do, and I can grab visual references from the internet. Do you have a specific picture of her you want me to use?"

Aldo reached for his phone and scrolled through a few images of Lola and the family from Thanksgiving, "Here, maybe this one?" he showed her a picture of a smiling Lola, with her arm around Aldo's waist.

"No, I have much better ones, look…"

"Now that's what I'm talkin' about! That one right there," he pointed to an image of Lola, in a three-quarter pose, lounging on a chair, in her kimono, the one embroidered with blue cranes and coral goldfish.

"Yes, I think this one's got the right pose and attitude, she looks relaxed and regal," Jesse agreed.

"Where'd you take that one?"

"In the art room. Lola agreed to come and model for my life drawing class one week. Which was about the only time they were ever on task," Jesse laughed.

"Okay, so I'll leave it in your capable hands now, if you need anything let me know, money for canvas, paints etc."

"It's okay, nonno, it's on me, the least I can do. Any time lines?"

"It'd be great if we could hang it by Easter week, that's when the season starts to pick-up and I'll want to show her off," Aldo said, smiling.

"That's four weeks from now, I think that's enough time, if I can get my canvas this week. I'll do my best nonno," Jesse said, kissing him on the cheek.

"I know you will, pussycat, and thanks. Now go, get that canvas, and leave the shallots to me."

FOUR WEEKS HENCE, Jesse, true to her promise, had finished the portrait, even finding, as if by magic, the right frame for it at a local antiques dealer, it was a fin-de-siècle, carved wooden frame, five inches deep, with gilded plaster acanthus leaf swags spanning the four corners. Now, it hung over the bar, loosely covered in paper, waiting for the unveiling.

Aldo had mixed-up a big pitcher of the lounge's new signature cocktail, the Lotini, composed of bourbon, splash of orange juice and ginger ale, a few drops of sweet kumquat liqueur, shaken over chipped ice, strained into a martini glass, and served with a thin spear of fresh ginger and an orange twist.

Nikos, Jesse, Voula and Aldo were standing by, watching the laptop for Nick and Lidia to log-in, joining the unveiling.

"Ah! Here they are!" Voula said, waving at the screen, Aldo and Jesse crowded in.

"Hi guys!" they greeted Nick and Lidia when another figure moved into view.

"Josh?" Jesse asked, surprised to see him.

Lidia answered, "Yes, Josh's rented your flat downstairs, and he's going to take care of the house and Pickles while we're in Italy. Isn't that great!" Lidia enthused.

"Yeah, great, good choice mom," Jesse said, feeling no enthusiasm whatsoever at the prospect of her ex taking over her digs, her house, her family, while she'll be stuck in the loft with Antonio.

"Okay!" Aldo said, standing by the painting, "Let's get this memorial going!" and with that, he pulled-off the paper to reveal a stunning figure of Lola, framed by an arbor of bougainvillea, reclining like an oriental odalisque on a red velvet chaise, in her yellow silk, embroidered kimono, a beaded mule dangling from one foot, a little spaniel in her lap, looking adoringly up at her. Her long, chestnut braids spilling over one shoulder, a lyre leaned against the chaise, symbol of Apollo, the Greek god of music.

Lola's dark, almond-shaped eyes regarded the viewer softly, a charming, self-satisfied smile, turning-up the corners of her coral lips. In the background, a rustic stone cottage, with a red wooden door, half-opened, inviting the viewer to enter. The work was painted in an impressionist style, broad, painterly brushstrokes, lots of dazzling dabs of sunlight and deep violet shadows.

"Wow Jess, that's beautiful," Josh said.

"Oh yes, great work, pussycat," Aldo said, giving her a bear hug, as the rest voiced their admiration, to a blushing Jesse.

"Ah, pardon me," came an upper-class, British voice from the doorway. "Sorry to intrude, but I'm meeting some friends, bit early, I'm afraid. Mind if I wait here in the lounge?"

"Of course," Aldo nodded to Nikos, who scurried to the door, showing the gentleman in. "Would you like to join our little celebration?" Aldo offered.

"Thank-you, most kind. What are you celebrating?" the man asked, as Aldo handed him a Lotini.

"The hanging of this portrait and the spirit of our beautiful, dear friend. To Lola!" Aldo raised his glass, as the others raised theirs, joining-in on the toast, the Toronto gang chiming-in with their prosecco, before signing-out.

"To Lola, then," the man took a sip of his drink. "Mm, that's nice, what do you call it?'

"The Lotini, bourbon, splash of orange juice and ginger ale," Aldo said, taking another sip.

"Yes, very nice, so's that picture," he took his glasses from his breast pocket and stepped-in for a closer look, "Hmm, yes, very handsome indeed. What do you want for it?"

"Oh, no it's not for sale. It's a memorial to our friend," Voula said.

"Oh dear, beg pardon. But may I ask who's the artist?"

"I am," Jesse said, stepping forward, "Jesse Ponti," she extended her hand.

He shook it, introducing himself, "Rear Admiral Harry Banfield, retired. My wife and I live on the island most of the year, winter in Bermuda. New here, are you?"

"Yes, my grandfather, Aldo Campanile, owns this restaurant," she said, pointing at Aldo, "I'm visiting for awhile from Canada."

"Lovely country, Canada, have friends in Victoria…So, you do portrait painting, eh?"

"No, not usually, my medium is collage, but yes, I paint and do some printmaking too, when the mood strikes me. At the moment, I'm on a sabbatical from teaching."

"Interested in taking-on a commission?"

"Maybe, depends what it is."

"The wife's always banging-on about not having a decent picture of the grandchildren, don't know why, not as if she doesn't know what they look like. Anyway, they're spending the summer with us, would you be interested in doing a group portrait at our place? It'd earn me lots of brownie points," he said, with a twinkle in his eye.

Nikos refreshed their glasses as Jesse thought for a moment, she found she was warming-up to this gentleman, he seemed like someone out of a P.G. Wodehouse novel, a little bumbling, sweet, but canny, nonetheless.

"I'll think about it, let you know after Easter," she said, smiling, not wanting to seem too eager for the job.

"Here's my card. Let me know what you've decided, I can pick you up anytime to survey the menagerie."

They shook hands again and the admiral departed to the terrace.

PASCAL CELEBRATIONS ON Corfu are one exuberant three-day pageant, beginning with the Epitaphios, on Good Friday, when every parish church processes with their funeral bier, accompanied by squads of choirs and marching bands. On Holy Saturday, the relics of Corfu's patron saint, Saint Spyridon, are paraded through the old town. Then, the ritual of the Second Resurrection is performed by throwing large amphorae from the balconies in the square, culminating in a feast to break the Lenten fast and a brilliant, evening fireworks display on The Esplanade. On Sunday, there is more feasting and a candlelight vigil, with yet more musical processions.

This Holy Saturday, after following the procession of Saint Spyridon's relics, Voula and Jesse joined the crush of spectators lining The Esplanade to witness the First Resurrection ritual.

"What's everyone waiting for Voula, the second coming?" Jesse asked, impatiently.

"Something like that. You see the people up there on the balconies, the ones with the *'botides'*, the amphorae?"

"Yeah, so?"

"Well, pretty soon, they're going to throw them

over, smash them to pieces. They're full of water, the water is released, just like the spirit of Christ was released upon his death. Water is the giver of life, in baptism, we accept Christ and his sacrifice, so that we may live eternally. At least, that's my Ukrainian Orthodox Sunday-school interpretation," Voula explained, turning with a smile towards Jesse.

"Sounds reasonable. The Orthodox Greek celebration is quite different from the Roman one I'm used to."

"Yes, I know, hunting for bunny rabbits' chocolate eggs. Now, in Ukraine –

"*Christos Anesti!*" interrupting Voula, the crowd suddenly roared, and applauded as the first amphora was smashed, then a second, and so on, down the line of the red-draped balconies, flying the blue and white Greek flag.

Just as the final amphora was tossed, in the shadow of where a curious Jesse had stepped, a hand reached out jerking her back.

"Hey!" Jesse shouted, annoyed, turning to its owner.

"Sorry, miss. I didn't mean to be rough, but you're too close to the firing line," the young man said in a soft, Boston accent, his deep-set, smoky grey eyes, bemused.

"Yeah, I guess I was," she conceded, regarding

the broken pottery shards near where she had stood.

"Oh well, you're welcome, anytime!" he shrugged.

"Sorry…thanks. I'm still a little startled," she said, rubbing her aching forearm.

"Let me see that," he took her arm. "Oops, guess I don't know my own strength, looks like a bruise is coming-on," he frowned, lightly stroking the bluish-red mark.

"Well, better a bruise than a concussion. I can put some ice on it, it shouldn't be too bad. Thanks again," Jesse said, withdrawing her arm, moving-on to a waving Voula.

"C'mon Jess, we need to find Aldo."

"Okay, I'm coming! Thanks again," she said hurrying away.

"Hey, wait! Are you staying in town?" the stranger, too late, shouted after her.

"Who was that Jess?" Voula asked.

"I dunno, didn't get his name, but he sure has a tough grip. Where is nonno anyway?"

"He should be waiting with the car, near the fort. We better get a move-on, it's nearly four o'clock,"

"What time are we supposed to be at Nikos'?"

"Four-thirty! I just hope Aldo got my text not to forget the chocolate bunnies, we ordered them specially from Canada. I don't want to disappoint the kids. They don't have the chocolate Easter-bunny tradition here, so we thought it would be fun," she said, hustling along, panting slightly from the effort.

"I'm sure he won't forget... Ah! there he is, by the car," Jesse said, waving to Aldo.

TO BREAK THE *Sarakosti*, the forty-day Lenten fast, Nikos' family, as all Corfiot Greeks, consumed generous bowls of magiritsa, a filling, delicious Easter soup, made of rice, lamb and leeks, topped with avgolemono, the traditional lemon-egg sauce. There were mezes and bowls of red-dyed, hard cooked eggs. The celebrants knocking their eggs against each other's, the one whose egg doesn't crack will have the best luck that year, Nikos' wife winning the round.

Then there was the sweet, rich, *fogatsa*, a domed, round brioche, scored with a cross, a legacy of four-hundred years of Venetian occupation. It was washed down with a choice of two kumquat liqueurs; a bright orange, sweet concoction, and the white variety, a bitter digestif made from the rind. The men favoured the bitter, the women indulged themselves with the sweet on ice, as well as nibbling from a plate of honey-almond biscuits and pistachio baklava, while the children broke into their lavishly iced, huge chocolate bunnies, anticipating the little novelty prizes secreted within.

They played with their treasures, traded them, argued, and fought over them, before settling down to the serious business of deciding which part of their rabbits to consume first.

Should one start from the ears, breaking-off the hard icing garnishes, putting them aside for last, or should one just bite off the nose or tail, devouring icing and chocolate in one go? After trying several approaches, some of Nikos' precocious off-spring decided that the best fun could be got out of pulling-off the icing, pelting each other with it, the non-combatants, using the opportunity to snatch each other's unguarded trinkets.

That is, until Nikos' wife confiscated all the chocolate bunnies, despite wining protests. Then she lined the miscreants up to roughly scrub the food, chocolate, and misery from their faces, in preparation for their trip to the Old Town, to watch the evening's fireworks.

Aldo, Voula and Jesse followed them in their car, luckily finding parking spaces not far from the Spianada Square, with a good outlook on the pyrotechnics. The children were excited and wanted to sit-up on the hoods of both cars, the adults, indulging them, watchfully.

Jesse decided to take a stroll around, to walk off the dinner and watch in silence, when she spied a familiar profile amidst a small group of revellers laughing and pointing at the brilliant, noisy display. She walked towards them and caught her rescuer's eye.

"Hey! Long-time, no see. How's the arm?" the broad-shouldered, tanned, dark-haired, young man greeted her warmly.

"Oh fine, it's okay, just needed a little ice…see," Jesse said, showing him her arm, smiling.

"Good! I'd hate to think I spoiled such a lovely limb, a lithe slip of willow," he said in mock gallant-ry, lightly kissing the inside of her forearm.

His friends laughed and made gagging noises. Jesse was a little uncomfortable, but flattered too, thinking her admirer had been partying a bit too much.

He turned towards his friends, introducing them, beginning with a lanky, blonde woman:

"Say hello to Suze, ah?…" he stopped and stared At Jesse.

"Jesse, Jesse Ponti," she said.

"Peter," he responded in kind, "Peter Olivera. And this," pointing back at the blonde, "is Suze Mahoney, roulette croupier, par excellence." Then going down the line, to the next woman, a short, buxom brunette, "this is her cousin, the estimable black-jack dealer, Charlene Mahoney, Charley for short, 'cause she is," he laughed, playfully punching her arm. "And this brute," Peter said, reaching-up to drape an arm around the thick neck of a hefty Samoan, "this is Tupe Malala, 'Wu Tang' to his friends, and ninja of the high-stakes poker table. Wu Tang, so named for his obsession with 'The Clan's' music." Wu Tang reached-out a big hand to Jesse.

Jesse judged Peter's crew to be in their late-twenties, and amiable. Suze tilted her head, twisting her long, straight hair in her fingers, while appraising Jesse, then said, "Hey Jesse, wanna join us on the yacht, we're just leaving to get a better view of the fireworks from the water and pop a few corks of bubbly," she smiled.

"Yes! C'mon, Jesse, it'll be fun, you gotta see this tub, it's fantastic!" Peter said.

"Your yacht?" Jesse asked.

"Ha! He only wishes," laughed Wu Tang, "The Medusa's where we work, and live, but it belongs to a Bulgarian, Boyana Aleksandrov, the real Medusa."

"Why 'Medusa'?" asked Jess, apprehensive.

"Because her wrath can turn strong men to stone!" shouted Charley.

"Oh yeah, weep at the thought of the Gorgon's

vengeance," warned Suze.

Peter looked at a worried Jesse, "C'mon guys, stop it, you're freaking her out!" Peter gently squeezed Jesse's shoulder, laughing. "Don't listen to them, they're just joking. Anyway, Medusa's away, so we all have a little time to play. Right?' he said, looking to his friends for affirmation.

"Really, it's fine, Jesse. Let's go before the fireworks are over," Suze said, making a move towards the road down to their tender.

"Yeah, and that Cristal isn't just gonna drink itself, is it?" Charley said, following her cousin.

"Okay!" Jesse decided, "I'll catch you-up in a sec, just have to tell my group I'm going."

"I'll go with you, Jesse. See you guys at the dock," Peter said, offering his arm to Jesse.

Aldo, sensing his granddaughter's approach, turned towards her.

"Nonno, this is Peter Olivera, I met him at the resurrection ceremony earlier, he saved me from being squashed," Jesse said, smiling.

Aldo extended his hand, "Aldo Campanile, pleased to meet you. Tourist, or expat?"

"Neither really. I'm working here, sort of," Peter said, a twinkle in his eye.

"What do you mean, 'sort of'?"

"Well, see that big black yacht out there, with all

the lights? That's where I live and work."

"What kind of work?"

"I'm an assistant staff manager."

"That's a big ship, how many souls do you assist in managing?'

"Nonno, he's not applying for a job!" Jesse was getting impatient.

"It's okay, Jesse. Fifteen. Her name's The Medusa, she's five-hundred and ninety feet, built in Riga, registered in Monaco," Peter said, with a little pride.

"Yes, and if we don't get a move on, we won't be able to see the fireworks from her decks. Right Peter?" Jesse nodded at him knowingly, pulling on his arm.

"Right, we better go, my friends are waiting. Nice to meet you Aldo," Peter said as Jesse turned to walk away, shouting over her shoulder, "Won't be too late! See you back at the house."

JESSE'S EYES WIDENED as she walked up the gangplank ahead of Peter; the yacht was immense, the brass fittings and teak railings gleamed, the deck floors glowed, all was immaculate. The lines of the ship were acutely angular, the stern was wide, the bow sharply tapered, rising at its apex, giving it an aerodynamic feel, as if the vessel could sprout wings and jettison-off, like a manta ray, over the water, at a moment's notice. They boarded on the port side of the poop-deck, where there was an open lounge, with bar, deck chairs, hot tub, and entertainment centre.

"This is the informal lounge, where my uncle Matt, who's the manager, lets us hang-out when la Medusa's not aboard and there's no guests. As you go up each deck, it gets crazier; the Gorgon's taste for luxury knows no bounds. On the third deck, is the beach club, with spa and swimming pool, just below the Helipad, on the top," he said pointing-up, "which converts to a lighted stage. But the best toy is the two-man submarine! The captain trained me on it, and we goof around in it when la Medusa's not here, pretend like we're Jacques and Philippe Cousteau."

"Wow! This is just like a floating luxury hotel, something out of a Bond movie," Jesse said in wonder, never having been on more than a day-sailing catamaran in the Caribbean.

"Peter laughed, "It *is* a floating luxury hotel."

Then taking her arm, he led her from the deck, through a pair of Art Nouveau gilt-framed, etched glass doors, depicting Caravaggio's Medusa. Against the left wall, near the entrance, sat an ebony bar, with leopard print bar stools on wrought iron legs. In the centre of the room, on the alabaster marble floor, edged in a black granite Greek-key motif, was a large, round, glass dining table on an elaborate brass cloisonné pedestal, surrounded by gilded, Italian cane furniture, with wide black and gold striped, silk cushions.

The décor exuded an opulent, Art Nouveau/Moroccan ambience, from the regal potted palms to the half life-size, ebony and brass black-a-moor lamp stands. They bordered the two large, silk, French tapestries depicting figures from Gustav Klimt's work, hung against the black, opalescent walls. There were four large, imposing, gold-flecked, Venetian chandeliers, hanging from the mirror-tile ceiling.

At the back of the room, beyond the dining-bar area, were brass-studded red leather pocket doors concealing a surround-sound, movie theatre that seated twelve, in red, hand-tooled Moroccan-leather club chairs.

Jesse's mouth hung open for a moment, she reached for her phone, holding it up to take a shot of the room, when Peter's hand came sharply down on hers, "Hey! What d'ya think you're doing?"

"I just wanted a shot for my Instagram, this room is fantastic. What's the issue?" Jesse said, a little angry.

"No pictures, no recordings. La Medusa is strict on her privacy. Understood?" he said, his hand still loosely on her wrist.

"Okay! Understood…guess I should've asked first." Then wanting to change the subject, and the atmosphere, she asked, "Hey, where's everyone else?"

"Below decks, in the bilge, where we Gollums usually live, when not working. They're bringing-up the champagne and caviar. Let's go grab a seat on the deck," he said, turning the lights off in the lounge.

"Cristal and caviar, eh? You guys must be really well-paid!" Jesse said, sitting down on a plush deck chair.

"We are, but that's a gratuity from the host of the last group we entertained."

"Really? Who was it…anyone famous?"

"A select group of high-stakes, hardcore players, mostly known in financial and UAE circles. The host was Hollywood, we all sign an NDA so can't name names, but his rhymed with Rooney."

Jesse went quiet, taking it all in. The view of the night sky from the stern, was a beautifully clear one to see the fireworks. She assumed that the higher decks were off-limits to staff, except for service, and so decided not to ask for a tour. As she settled back and wondered at this fabulous night, the exotic yacht, the glorious fireworks, and the handsome man beside her, she felt a little bit in heaven.

"Hey Peter, comfortable enough? Geeze you could've given us a hand!" Suze said as she emerged from the semi-circular, smoked glass and chrome elevator, onto the poop deck, bearing a tray of gravlax, caviar and crackers.

Wu Tang and Charley followed behind her with a service tray and four bottles of Cristal Champagne.

"In case you haven't noticed, we have a guest to entertain. Anyway, what's the big deal, just slap a few nibbles together, and bring some drinks up," Peter scoffed.

"Fine! Don't notice the trouble I took in styling these canapés, the clusters of grapes, the dill fronds, the artfully scattered caper berries, to say nothing of the fancily twisted lemon spirals," Charley protested, laughing.

"It looks lovely, Charley, thanks," Jesse said, as Charley handed her a cocktail napkin, with two of her creations.

"Take no notice of Charley's complaining, Jesse, she's a frustrated restaurateur," advised Peter, taking several canapés from the tray.

"Really? My grandfather runs a restaurant on the island, The Asteri, in Gouvia, in Kontokaly Bay."

"Is that where you work?" asked Charley.

"No, I'm on unpaid sabbatical from teaching, so

I'm just figuring-out what I'm going to do while sponging-off my granddad," Jesse said, with a little laugh.

"You're not Greek, are you?" Wu Tang asked, handing her a glass of champagne.

"No, I'm Italian-Canadian, from Toronto, but my grandad is originally from a village near Pescara, and dad's family is Calabrese."

"Pescara? No way! That's where my family's from, we emigrated to Boston when I was thirteen," said Peter, holding-up his glass for a refill.

"That explains it! I couldn't place your accent, I can hear the Boston in some words, but then Italian too, especially when you roll your 'r's'a little and-a, put-a a little tag-a on some words," she said, mocking him gently.

"Oh! I tot I no do-a dat-a anymorrra!" he laughed.

"C'mon, I didn't make you feel self-conscious, did I? I like your hybrid accent, it's kinda cute," Jesse said, nudging him in the arm.

"Cute? Ha! You should hear him in full-tantrum English, yelling at the wait staff, eh Suze," Charley said.

"Oh yeah…" Suze stood-up. "You, yeah, you – Chloe is it? Or is it 'Clueless'? cause that's what you are," she pointed at an empty chair. "Do you even know what silver service is? No? Well let me demonstrate," Suze pulled-out an imaginary napkin, "Never, ever, drop a napkin in the lap of a guest, or touch them, especially not the Sultan of Dubai. You do this," she turned around gracefully and with a flourish mimed draping it over Peter's lap. "And don't make eye contact with, or speak directly to, any titled guest, got it? 'Cause if you drop napkins, touch laps, or speak, I'll chop-off your fingers, slice-off the tip of your tongue, and feed it all to the Gorgon's pet shark!"

Charley and Wu Tang bent over laughing; Jesse couldn't help but join-in too.

Peter shifted in his seat, cleared his throat, and said, "Well, I'm not as bad as 'Herr Alfonse', he's a real martinet."

"Bullshit!" Charley countered, "you're as bad as each other."

"Who's 'Herr Alfonse'?" Jesse asked.

"He's Chief Steward, and chief snitch on all serving staff, Mussolini here, is 'da Po-po', it be his fave part of the job," pointing to Peter, Wu Tang smiled broadly, flashing two gold-clad, upper canines.

"Never mind the character assassination, just open another bottle, will ya, Wu-Tang?" Peter said.

"Coming-up boss, defending your rep is sure thirsty business," he said popping a cork.

Just then, a huge burst of fireworks lit-up the sky with a bang, each colorful cascade unfolding with a whistle and ending in a sprinkle of crackling stars. The group fell silent, their attention diverted to the brilliant show, holding them in childlike wonder for several minutes, as fireworks always seem to, no matter the spectator's age.

In fact, they were so enthralled with the spectacle, they failed to hear the approach of Matt Olivera, Peter's uncle, boss, and manager.

"What's this, kids? Holding a party without me?" he said, startling them.

Peter, rising quickly, spoke, "Oh hey! I didn't know you were aboard. I thought you were on shore, 'seeing a man about a dog'. Wu," he snapped his fingers, "get Uncle Matt a glass of bubbly."

Matt looked around, his eyes settling on Jesse, "And who's this vision?"

"Oh, a lady in distress I rescued earlier. Uncle Matt, meet Jesse Ponti," he nodded towards Jesse, as he stepped aside to let his uncle sit down.

"Matt Olivera, Jesse. Pleased to meet you," he said taking her hand in his large hirsute grip.

"Like wise, Mr. Olivera," Jesse said, a little non-plussed as he took Peter's seat, close beside her.

As he accepted a glass of champagne from Wu Tang, Matt said, "And what kind of distress did my nephew rescue you from?"

"Oh, just from being crushed by a flying amphora water-bomb."

"Got a little too close to the action, eh?" he chuckled, taking a sip of bubbly.

The group, no longer relaxed and jolly, seemed tense and alert. Peter stood stiffly against the railing next to Wu Tang, Charley and Suze sat upright, as if waiting for orders.

"Matt, would you like a caviar canapé?" Charley offered.

"Thank-you Charley, but I'll pass. Have to watch the sodium intake," then turning to their guest, asked, "tell me Jesse, what brings you to Corfu?"

"A sabbatical from teaching. Just needed a reset, and since my grandad has a place here, and graciously offered to put up with me for awhile, I thought I'd come and explore," Jesse said, nodding appreciatively, as Wu Tang refilled her glass.

"And that's the craziest coincidence, Uncle Matt. You'd never guess where her nonno's from," Peter said.

"Uh…Pescara?"

"How'd you know?" Peter asked.

"Well, she doesn't sound like she's from Boston, but her last name ends in a vowel, so Dr. Watson, I deduced it must be Italy. Where in Italy I ask myself, we might have in common? Pescara! It's not hard to figure out kid, you don't need a college degree," Matt scoffed, leaning back, self-satisfied, draining his glass.

Peter blanched at his uncle's admonition, made worse in that it was in front of his crew, and his guest. He felt like a fool, but tried to recover the situation, "Actually, it was kind'a rhetorical…Jesse's obviously Italian."

Ignoring Peter's feeble riposte, Matt continued, "Where in Pescara?"

"In the province of Chieti, in Vasto. I've never been there, but I've seen pictures, it looks beautiful," Jesse responded, Peter seemed as if he was dying to speak, but held his tongue, "I'd love to go there, I don't think there's family left though. And you, Matt?"

Matt, who had grinned and nodded at the mention of Vasto, said, "Now that, young lady, *is* an astounding coincidence, the Oliveras are from Vasto too. We are paesani. What's your nonno's name?"

"Aldo, Aldo Campanile, I doubt if you'd know him, he left decades ago for Canada, and has never returned to Italy."

This time, Matt raised his eyebrows and stared intently at Jesse, grasping her arm, "Aldo Campanile? On Corfu? I can't believe it!"

Wu Tang refilled his glass and topped-up the others, who sat quietly looking-on.

"How do you know him?" Jesse asked.

"We grew up together, were best friends, until the accidents."

"Accidents? What accidents?" Jesse furled her brow, looking at Matt with concern.

Matt sat back and considered his response… "Ask your nonno," then looking at his watch added, "it's late, so drink-up boys and girls. Peter, you can take your 'damsel in distress' home now, and the rest of you clean-up. I want this deck immaculate. And don't just take the party below decks, meeting 8:30 sharp, tomorrow!"

Turning to shake Jesse's hand, he said, "It was a pleasure to meet you, young lady. Please tell Aldo that Matt Olivera from Vasto, sends his regards."

"I will, Matt. Goodnight," Jesse said rising, "and thanks guys for inviting me and sharing your champagne, you must come to the Asteri for lunch sometime, on me."

"I don't think we'll get shore leave again for at least a week, la Medusa's got an important group coming on Tuesday, but take care, and we'll see you again," Suze said, the rest of the group, echoing her sentiment.

THE NEXT MORNING, Aldo and Voula were on the terrace having breakfast and making plans for the season, when Jesse, still in her pyjamas, appeared.

"Morning Jess, want some coffee?" Voula said, rising to get her a mug.

"Thanks, Voula," she said listlessly, sitting down, across from Aldo.

"And what time did you get in?" he asked, arching an eyebrow.

"Not too late, around midnight, and no, I'm not hung-over, only had a couple of glasses of champagne."

"That baggage tells another story," he laughed, making circles around her eyes.

"No, really nonno, I got back fairly early and *wasn't* partying til dawn. I just couldn't sleep…all night, tossing and turning," she grimaced, taking the hot mug from Voula.

"Something on your mind then, Jess? Want me to do some tarot for you after? It helps bring to the surface subconscious issues, and literally, 'puts them on the table' to be dealt with," Voula said, spreading cream cheese on a toasted bagel, and handing it to Aldo.

"Nah, it's okay, nothing I can't handle, Voula. Thanks anyway. I know what's bugging me," she replied, stirring a spoon of sugar into her coffee.

"Care to share?' Aldo asked, biting into his bagel.

"Well, some of it's kinda' personal, but the rest of it's financial. While I was awake, I came up with a plan to make some money and keep busy, without taking a job from a local," Jesse said, taking a warm bagel from Voula, and cutting it in half.

"So, what's the plan, pussycat?" Aldo asked, getting-up to make more coffee.

"I thought I'd put my art training to use, first by accepting a commission from Admiral Banfield, and second, by offering two-week plein-air sketching and watercolor workshops. You know, visit the natural beauty spots around this bay. Then some watercolor, or pastel work around the Old Town, churches, piazzas, fountains, ruins, you know the 'genre' thing."

"Sounds good, have you given any thought to the details?" Aldo said, as he refilled everyone's mug.

"Yeah, some. The students can purchase their own stuff from the art supply store in town, I just have to talk to the proprietor, see what they will stock, availability, prices, etc. maybe even swing a small discount, if the numbers warrant. It's just basic stuff they'll need, so it should be fine.

"I have to decide what to charge, I think keeping the courses flexible will be good, each of the two weeks is a complete module, so students can sign-up for just one week and have a finished work or go on to more advanced work in the second, if they're really into it. So, I'll likely end-up with mixed-level classes.

"I need a place where we can meet every morning, just for an hour or so before heading-out, to go over last session's work and demonstrate techniques. I'll also need to get brochures and some posters printed-up. And last, but not least, I'll need to rent transport, like a motor scooter…which may require my taking a small loan from 'Nonno's Bank and Grill'," she said, smiling broadly at Aldo.

"No problem, just let me know how much, and if your group meets between eight and ten, you can use the restaurant terrace, but the kitchen will be closed, no catering! And you gotta be out by ten, firm, leaving it as you found it, okay?"

"Okay! Thanks, nonno…love ya!" she smiled, and blew him a kiss.

"Yeah, yeah," he laughed, taking another bagel.

"So, Jess, any plans for today? Want to go with us to Parga to see the Venetian castle and visit the oracle at Ephyra? We're catching the ferry in an hour…" Voula offered.

"Um no, I have plans. Peter…you know, from yesterday…well he's asked me to go on a beach picnic with him," Jesse said, rising quickly, to take her mug and plate to the dishwasher.

"Oh, has he now? Well, just watch yourself with that guy, he's a bit too smooth for my liking," Aldo warned.

"He's fine, a perfect gentleman," she replied, slightly annoyed. Then turning to leave, she stopped at the doorway, "Oh, I nearly forgot to tell you nonno. I met his uncle on the yacht, a Matt Olivera from your hometown, Vasto? He says to give you his regards."

Aldo suddenly looked worried, Voula looked at him sideways, not sure what to make of the apprehension she felt.

"Who's this Matt Olivera, Aldo? You've never mentioned him before," Voula asked warily.

"Matt? Why should I mention him? He's a nobody from my past. Hey, how many nobodies from your past you've never mentioned, eh?" he challenged.

"Whoa, don't get so defensive. It was an innocent question, if you don't want to tell me, just say so, and civilly, if you please," Voula said firmly, rising to clear the breakfast table.

"Sorry," he said, reaching out for her hand, "it's

just that the past, in Vasto, is not a place I want to revisit, okay?"

She leaned-over to kiss his cheek, "Okay, the matter's closed. Now let's get ready to go see that oracle."

Chapter Three

SUMMER

I T WAS NEARLY noon as Jesse made her way to the marina beside the Asteri, looking for the tender with a black and gold Medusa insignia. She stood at the landing dock, shading her eyes from the bright sunlight, scanning the boats moored there, when she caught sight of him, shouting and waving to her from the deck of a small sailboat.

"Ahoy there, Lassie! Care to go for a spin around The Horn?" Peter mugged in his cartoon imitation of an old sailor.

"Sure! As long as I'm back for dinner," she laughed as he took her hand, helping her on to the deck. "Where did you get this boat?" she asked looking around the Fareast 18 daysailer.

"I chartered it for the day, I wanted a smaller vessel, a little Catalina, but this is all they had. Still, it's easy enough for one-hand to rig and launch. And she's fast," he said, pointing to the sail, "has a square-top, fully battened mains'l and a sprit-flown spinnaker – good for racing.

"Take the rudder off, retract the keel, she'll float in one foot of water. Handy, as we're going to moor close to a nice, secluded beach I know," he said, jumping on to the dock, untying the mooring line, tossing it on to the deck, before jumping back aboard.

"Well, sure sounds like you know your way around sailboats. I'll bet you know how to tie all those fancy knots too," Jesse said, taking some sunscreen from her bag, applying it to her arms and legs.

"The one knot every sailor needs, is the most simple and elegant – the bowline," which Peter pronounced as 'bolin'. "Holds anything fast, quick and easy to untie. Now, take a seat, and we'll get underway."

As they motored out of the marina to the open water, where there was a good breeze from the east, just enough to luff the sail and take them along at a nice steady pace, Jesse asked, "Where are we going? And what have you planned for lunch, I'm starving."

Peter put on the auto pilot, then disappeared into the cabin, coming-up with a cooler, putting it on the seat between them, he opened the lid, and handed her a wrapped sandwich, "I hope you like lobster."

"Love it!" Jesse said, quickly unwrapping the treat.

"Good, cause my version of a lobster roll is the best in Boston. My secret's finely chopped chives and celery, a good squirt of lemon, shake of hot sauce and Old Bay seasoning in a dollop of mayo, bib lettuce, and a big buttery croissant," he said, popping the cork on a bottle of champagne, filling two glasses for them.

"Don't tell me that's more Cristal," Jesse said, taking her glass.

"Actually, it's the last bottle, so Suze and Charley will be pissed… Salute!" Peter grinned, tipping his glass to Jesse's.

After she took a sip, and a bite of her sandwich, she closed her eyes, raised her face to the sun and sighed, "Oh, this is *tooo* nice."

"Mmhm…" he agreed, from a mouthful of sandwich. Then, washing it down with a gulp of bubbly, stifling a burp, he said, "don't get too impressed, there's more good stuff to come."

"Okay, where's our first stop?" Jesse said, pouring them some more wine.

"Actually, I thought we'd sail north around the top of the island to the west coast; then south, down to the caves at Paleokastritsa. We have masks and flippers to explore into the grottoes a little, that is if you're a snorkeller."

"Yes, and a good swimmer, got all my badges at

summer camp," Jesse said, digging into the cooler, finding another lobster-croissant. She passed half to Peter. "I haven't been to the west coast yet, but have heard about the caves," Jesse said enthusiastically.

"After that, we can hike up to the monastery, and to Bella Vista, it's a look-out with stunning views. Then, there's Agios Spiridon, where I know a little beach, tucked away in a secluded lagoon, where we can swim and sunbathe. There's a good fish restaurant around there too, we can grab something, maybe calamari, I like their grilled octopus too," he said, wiping a drop of mayo from the corner of his mouth.

"Oh, I love grilled octopus, with plenty of garlic and oregano. I can smell the charcoal now, I don't know why, but snorkelling always makes me ravenous."

"Good," Peter grinned, as he reached into the cooler for some bottled water, "if you want to change, or need a washroom, just go down into the cabin." He pulled-off his tee shirt, and grabbed Jesse's sun lotion, "Would you mind?" he said turning his back to her.

"Sure," she said, spreading the cool lotion across and down his warm, tanned, muscular back, noticing a tattoo on his left shoulder, a crucifix atop a circle of thorns, surrounded on the outside by ten black dots, on the inside of the circle, were three red drops of blood. 'What's the 'tat' about?" she asked, running her index finger around the circle.

He shuddered a little, and said, "Just something from my misspent youth. And you…do you have any?"

"Only one…a postage-stamp of the Canadian flag, on my lower back, just above my butt cleavage. I thought it was funny, you know, kinda 'Return to Sender'. I got it when I was sixteen, underage, but my friends knew this woman who'd do it anyway. My parents never knew, they would've had fits!"

"My parents aren't quite so protective, they cut me loose at twenty-two, when I dropped-out of MIT, giving-up my scholarship. Kicked me out, and that was that."

"Really? I've kind of dropped-out too, had a teaching contract, and a nice, steady, boyfriend. Everything, neat and secure, tied-up just like a 'bolin', then like that," she snapped her fingers, "I undid it all, but my family never cut me loose because of it. They're good that way."

"That's nice, to be a rebel with a safety net."

"What do you mean? What's wrong with having a supportive family?" Jesse asked feeling defensive.

"Nothing, in principle. In practice though, it just delays your growing-up, knowing that you always have a fall-back. I'll bet you have permanent digs in your parent's basement, don't you?" Peter smirked arching an eyebrow.

"Well, I did until my ex took it over at my parent's behest. Now, I've gotta bunk with my infant brother in the loft," Jesse said, folding her arms, indignantly.

"Oh wa-wa, princess! Has to bunk with her baby brother," Peter mocked, sticking-out his lower lip.

Jesse laughed at his funny face, but nevertheless felt a little disconcerted by the truth. "So, tell me, 'Mr. Hard-Knocks School of Life', what's your rebel's story?" Jesse challenged.

"I was rescued from terminal security, or should I say, 'Shanghaied' by Uncle Matt, the black sheep of the family. He saw I was really unhappy fulfilling my parents' expectations and social ambitions, had none of my own. So, knowing how much I love sailing and the sea, offered me a job with la Medusa," he said, standing-up to start manually steering the craft.

"But I did have to start at the bottom, worked in all the stations, housekeeping, food service, learned the protocols of running a luxury craft. They even sent me to a school that trains staff for this market. Then, the step-up to the exclusive casino club and assistant manager, under Uncle Matt, Manager of Operations."

"And the crew, the guys who actually run the ship? What about them?"

"That's the captain's bailiwick, I don't touch that. They, and security, answer directly to la Medusa."

"And the kitchen staff?"

"The chef manages the day to day, menus, budget, but liaises with me, orders come from top down, through me to him. The same with Alfonse."

"So, this casino, is that how La Medusa makes her money?"

"It's not so much the money she makes there, although, she does well, it's her connections, that in turn make her the real money. And don't ask me how, let's just say her interests are diversified in an extremely competitive, lucrative field," he said, turning to flash her a smile.

"Oh, sorry, didn't mean to pry," Jesse said, putting on her sunglasses, leaning back on the banquette.

"No, that's okay. It's good you're interested, 'cause I have a proposition for you."

"Yeah? What's that?"

"Come here and I'll tell you."

Jesse got up and stood beside Peter.

"Here, take the wheel, hold her at three o'clock, good, just like that."

Jesse did as she was told, the wheel felt warm and

a little moist from his grip.

"So, what's the proposition?"

"How would you like to work evenings, as hostess in the casino? Had to let ours go last week. She was unreliable, and too familiar with the guests. But I think you'd be perfect, good-looking, classy, well-spoken, smart. What do you say?"

"Well, I'm not sure, I've never worked as hostess before, let alone in a casino environment, with celebrities."

"It's not rocket science; I'll show you what to do. Part of the time, I'll be on the floor with you, when I'm not, you can summon me from your blue tooth, and there's surveillance monitors too.

"Most of the clientele are ladies and gentlemen, but I can't lie, a few are assholes. I'm sure you can handle them, just like you're handling this boat," he said, rubbing her shoulders. "And the money and tips are great. La Medusa's generous, all she asks in return is be loyal, be quiet and do your job well."

"Sounds good, but I'm assuming I'll need some pretty formal attire, which I didn't bring with me."

"No worries, there's a few upscale boutiques in town, I'll take you shopping tomorrow afternoon. I'll get you something appropriate, it won't take much to make you look the part, you look great already," he said, planting a warm kiss on the base of her neck.

Jesse smiled and felt a little silly, falling for a cheesy line, but he was so charming… "Okay! You've made me an offer I just can't refuse."

WHEN THEY FINALLY made it to their first destination, Peter dropped anchor near the mouth of Nafsika's Cave.

Sunlight illuminated its natural minerals, lighting the water with fluorescent shades of turquoise. Into this pool of magic light Jesse swam, feeling like one of the maenad's, devotees of Dionysus, imagining this as his aqueous temple, where his sensual mysteries were performed.

Peter followed her into the ethereal grotto, transfixed by the schools of exotic fish, chameleons whose colors, dark and intense one minute, by changing direction, led by a singular mind into the light, transformed into psychedelic flashes of sparkling jewels.

When the grotto narrowed, and they could go no further, Jesse followed Peter out to the boat. Exhilarated, she mounted the ladder, grabbed a towel from the bench, and tossed another to an emerging Peter.

Jesse dried-off quickly, her back to her companion, as she dropped her towel, she felt his around her waist, drawing her toward him. She turned, he kissed her brown shoulders, her throat, working-up to her warm, soft mouth.

They never made it to the monastery at Bella Vista and the lookout's stunning views, another time perhaps. They did dine on smoky, moist, octopus, crisp calamari and drank tangy, refreshing retsina at Agio Spiridon, then swam naked in a nearby secluded lagoon. They lay silent, entwined, on the toasted sand, when the crimson sky beckoned them to depart, the west wind filling their sails, the warmth of the setting sun at their backs, they headed home, into the waxing moon.

AN UNEXPECTED VISITOR

"Aldo!" Voula called from the terrace entrance, into the bar, "there's someone here to see you."

"Who?"

"A Matt from Vasto, I think he's the one Jesse–

Before she could finish her sentence, an impatient Matt walked past her, booming at Aldo, "Paesan! So good to see you! It's been too long!" He made to greet his old friend with the traditional kiss on both cheeks, when Aldo backed away, extending his hand instead. "Oh, Americano, eh?" Matt, unperturbed shook his friend's hand.

"Canadese, actually," Aldo said, unsmiling.

"Same continent, same manners, well, almost," Matt said with a chuckle. "I've spent some years in Boston, myself, but am really a global citizen these days."

"Yeah, Jesse, my granddaughter said," Aldo nodded.

"Lovely girl." Then looking around asked, "Um, Aldo, can an old friend get a drink around here?"

Aldo replied, reluctant to be too welcoming, "Let's go to the bar, what's your pleasure?"

"Join me in a beer. It's pretty quiet, I'm sure you can spare the time, take a break, catch-up on hometown gossip," Matt said sliding onto a bar stool. "Nice place you've got here," he said, looking around after taking a sip of his beer.

"We like it, just getting it back on its feet, Greece's economy, being what it is."

"Good opportunity for the right investors though. Like me and my associates, we're looking for opportunities around here."

"I thought you were working for that Bulgarian, Boyana Aleksandrov, the one they call 'la Medusa'."

"I am, I'm her right-hand man, but this is a side-hustle, my retirement fund," Matt winked, taking another sip of beer.

"I think it's too slow for you around here, have to be in it for the long-haul to see real returns," Aldo said, not having his drink, eyeing Matt keenly.

"Those buildings, next door, they're yours too?"

"Part of the business, yes. Six housekeeping units, under construction. But we have four finished guest suites upstairs. That's all for now. In time, we plan to direct the profits to expanding on this cove, as demand warrants."

"Great idea, beautiful spot, marina next door, sandy beaches on the other side, definitely has potential. Why wait for profits to come in before you expand, when my associates and I can inject some cash right now? We have people in construction, Romanian, can get it up in no time. And suppliers, I can get you better deals, guaranteed, than what your current chain gives," Matt said, his eyes lighting-up.

"What? No, we like our suppliers and the pace we've planned, and don't need help from you. Listen paesan, you can keep your filthy money, I know where it comes from." Aldo leaned forward, a little menacingly.

Matt laughed, "Oh, do you now? Well, then you should know someone's gotta do the laundry!"

"It's not going to be me, clear? Anyway, this isn't my establishment alone, I've got partners," Aldo said, running a cloth over the bar.

"So? You're a pretty persuasive guy, tell them a story to bring them around. You're good at stories."

"What's that supposed to mean?" Aldo said warily.

"Like the story you told me about the unfortunate, fatal accidents, both your parents had. You told me you cleaned those floors, didn't leave any grease for your mom, then your dad to slip on. Quite the coincidences, I believed you, but no one else in that town did. You know it's still an open case?"

"Who says?"

"My god son, Gaetano, Chief of Police. Bright guy, ambitious, would look good on him to solve a cold case. Your dad was popular with his old buddies in the force, they never forget."

"Well, you and they can forget that. It is a closed case, as far as I'm concerned. I told you the truth, I don't care who says different!" Aldo, said, banging down his fist, angry now.

"But you must admit, didn't look good your running away, stealing all the cash from your dad's safe first. Do you know, there's no statute of limitations on murder in Italy? They have an extradition treaty with Greece too," Matt sneered.

"I did nothing wrong; I ran because the whole town was against me from the get-go. You're right, my dad's buddies wanted a scapegoat, I wasn't going to oblige. They turned a blind eye to my mother's blackened ones for years, I just got sick of being his punching bag too," Aldo turned his back on his guest and began slicing lemons.

"Tell it to the Questura, my friend," Matt countered, threatening the probity of Italy's provincial police.

Aldo turned on him, paring knife in hand, "Get out of here, before I do commit murder!"

"Cool down, paesan. I'll wait on the terrace for Jesse, I'm here to pick her up for her first shift," he smiled malevolently.

"She's not working for you, I'll forbid it!"

"Really? She's an adult, perhaps she'd like to hear the story too? Anyway, you think it over, then I'll pay you another visit. In good time, no pressure, but I guarantee, you'll come around." With that, he left his business card on the bar and waited outside, standing on the terrace, arms behind his back, plotting, taking in the charming view.

"JUST LOOK AT that. Right on top of it, she's a natural, punters like her too," Matt said, eyeing Jesse's progress as she greeted the guests, and worked the room, making sure the wait staff was 'on the ball'.

"Told you she'd be brilliant," Peter grinned, self-satisfied, watching his protégée from the sidelines.

"You done good kid." Matt patted him on the shoulder.

"Thanks. Now, how'd you make out with the old man? Is he simpatico?"

"Not just yet, but I'll get him there, leverage is all it takes. And I've got two levers, his dark past, and his bright, present, granddaughter. So, one way or another, we'll be his partners. But you stay well in the background, say nothing, show no interest in his business, only in the granddaughter, got it?"

"Got it, that's one job I can do all day and night."

Jesse, aware of the surveillance, and approving nods she was getting from her bosses, smiled broadly as she swept around the room, making sure no guest went thirsty, no soiled coasters or full ashtrays were in sight. That the wait staff had plenty of pristine, warm, mint-scented hand towels to refresh the guests, and that those seeking a quiet spot to smoke a cigar or enjoy a snifter were comfortably ensconced in the cigar lounge, and well-supplied from the bar and walk-in thermidor, cigar smoking being forbidden on the floor.

She was also responsible for checking on the staff serving guests on the deck lounge, that the music was low and to their liking, and that staff were attentive with food and drink orders. No dirty plate, glass or empty serving tray sat for more than a minute, before being cleared. If it wasn't, she had only to raise her hand, snap her fingers and point in the offender's direction.

It surprised her how quiet the players were, the intense atmosphere of concentration, highly charged with energy, but hushed as a library, which added to its mystique. The rare, boisterous patron was managed quickly and expertly by Peter and Matt. If anyone really got out of hand, there was always security ready to swiftly usher them out and into the elevator, to the 'quiet room', where they were given cold, sparkling mint-water and 'encouraged' to compose themselves, before being escorted off the vessel.

Even though her calves and feet were aching from standing in heels for most of her ten-hour shift, breaks excepted, she felt exhilarated, only twenty-minutes to go, until she was off. She had been keen to make a great impression on Peter and the guests.

He promised that in time, depending on her performance, she could begin switching shifts with Michaela, the senior hostess, currently working the exclusive high-rollers suite.

Apparently, these were the beluga caviar and Christal tipping patrons; she couldn't imagine the stakes they must be playing for, as judging by the familiar faces, designer clothes, bling, and stack of chips of her current patrons, there was some serious wealth, or at least crazy good credit in the room.

As she raised her hand to indicate service was needed at one of the blackjack tables, Peter came up behind her, and whispered in her ear, "So, Cinderella, ready to return to your pumpkin?"

"But boss, I have twenty minutes left, I hope you're not showing me any favoritism," she quietly laughed back.

"Not a chance. Matt will take over now, he wants to circulate, greet the newcomers, connect with the regulars, before last orders."

"Good, I'll just get my kit from the staff lounge. Won't be long, just want to change my shoes and grab some water, meet you on the poop deck."

As they sped along, the inky-black satin water below her, the indigo, star-studded sky above, Jesse breathed-in the salty air, and couldn't stop smiling. Snuggling close to her exciting companion, she felt she'd never really been alive until now, when it suddenly seemed everything was possible, the world her oyster, and dull, little Toronto, a lifetime away.

As Peter tied the tender to the dock, and helped Jesse up, she said, "I'm okay from here, go back, get some sleep." She kissed him deeply.

"You sure? I see Aldo's left the lights on for you, hope he's not waiting-up to give you grief," Peter said, his arms around her waist.

"No. Anyway, just let him try, it's my life," she said, kissing him again. "Huh, it's funny. I feel like I'm doing the 'walk of shame', when truth is, I just put in a hard night's work!" she laughed. Slinging her kit over her shoulder, she waved her lover good-bye.

"WHAT'S ALL THIS?" Aldo asked Voula, as he unrolled a wad of twenty, and fifty-dollar bills, wrapped-up in his napkin.

"Jesse. Must've left it last night. She came in really late, around two-thirty," Voula said, standing at the stove making scrambled eggs.

Aldo turned the napkin over, to read the message

written in lipliner, 'For room and board', smiley face. "Huh, must've done well last night. Hope she doesn't get addicted to the money and the attention," Aldo said glumly.

"Why shouldn't she like the money and attention, gloomy guts?" Voula challenged, plunking his eggs down before him.

"Because I don't like the people she's involved with. That Peter is a player, and I don't mean cards!" Aldo said, vigorously shaking pepper on his eggs.

"Really? Well, I thought your issue would be more with our recent visitor, that Matt, from Vasto. I've done some tarot on him; High priestess and the Tower keeps coming up. Also, six of cups, the three and seven of swords. So, what past secret has he got on you that could shake your world?"

"No secret, woman, keep that hocus pocus for your clients," he said, biting noisily into a crisp piece of toast.

"Bullshit, Aldo! Tarot doesn't lie, I got the Devil card too, you fear this Matt...why? Better tell me now. I can help you. Trust me?" She put a hand on his shoulder.

Aldo put down his fork, considered for a moment, then relented. "Okay, you're right. I do fear him and that nephew, a little, and not for me. For what I'm afraid they're getting Jesse into.

"Matt always had a bad reputation in Vasto, his whole family were connected in every way, bank, politics, police, merchant's association, even the church. It was an open secret, go to them for help, they have you by the nuts forever! I think my dad, always short of money, got mixed-up with them. Bad seed, all of them. As for secrets of mine? Ha! Matt has more secrets than a Buddhist has past lives!"

Voula withdrew her hand, and rested it beneath her chin, eyeing Aldo for a few moments when, finally, she spoke, "So, what are you going to do to protect your granddaughter?"

"Not sure. Do you want this?" he said pushing his plate away, "I'm not very hungry." With that he got up to go.

"Where are you going? It's Monday, our only day off, thought we'd do something together, go to the beach maybe?"

"I need to take a walk, alone, on the mountain. I'll be back in a couple of hours, we can do something then, okay?" he gave her a kiss, before departing.

Frowning, Voula sat down to finish the eggs, and do some thinking on how she might help with Jesse.

After clearing-up the breakfast dishes, Voula decided to attend to her flowers and herbs on the terrace. She filled the watering can, snips in hand, set about watering and dead heading her profuse, container garden.

Dead-heading was a favorite meditative activity for her, along with pruning; concentration on the mundane task at hand occupied her present mind, allowing her subconscious to enter a zone, where it dove deep, then emerged into her consciousness with a solution, or at least, advice. After twenty minutes or so, some enlightenment was emerging, when she was interrupted by Jesse.

"Morning, Voula!" Jesse said, brightly.

"Oh, you startled me, didn't expect to see you until noon, at least."

"My room faces east, it's too bright in there, I wish nonno would get my shutters fixed. Anyway, I feel good," she said, stretching-out on one of the lounges. "The garden looks great, so vibrant." Jesse said, looking around at the commanding canna lilies, giant crotons, exotic gingers, geraniums, and petunias. Even the bushy, variegated ferns, and brilliant begonias, shouted from the shade of the pergola.

"Thanks, I think it's coming along," she responded, getting-up from her crouch, straightening her back. "I forget how much energy the young have. In Kiev, I used to go out dancing until midnight, on to an after-hours club 'til dawn, then home for coffee, a shower and off to work! Catch-up with sleep on the weekends," Voula laughed.

"Well, I wasn't out dancing 'til dawn, I was working, and it's harder work than you'd think. You have to be everywhere at once, keep the guests happy, make sure service doesn't lag as the evening winds down, everybody's gotta be up and perky. Don't know how Peter and the rest do it. It's pretty hard on the feet too!" she said, flexing her toes.

"But it's good money. I saw the roll you left for Aldo, that was generous of you," Voula smiled, and sat on the edge of the lounge, taking Jess' foot in hand, she began to massage her arch.

"I owe it to him, and I want to pay my way… ooh, that feels good," Jesse said, relaxing her foot.

"Tell me about the boat, this floating pleasure palace, must be pretty glamorous," Voula said, taking her other foot.

"Oh my god, yes! Voula, I've never seen anything like it, and at night everything sparkles, including the guests, I felt like I walked onto a set from that Bond movie, Casino Royale. Only the guys aren't in tuxedos."

"Too bad, I love a man in a tuxedo," Voula sighed.

"Oh, me too. But that can be dangerous, single girl rule is, never hook-up with one at a wedding or other formal affair, wait to size him up in jeans, in the daylight. They may look like Prince Charming in their tux but turn out to be a frog in a hoodie."

"So girl, just hook-up with the magic, dance with the Prince, ditch the frog in the morning," Voula laughed. "Now, tell me about this la Medusa, what she like? Scary as they say she is?"

"Don't know yet, she hasn't deigned to meet a plebe like me, but I'd sure like to meet her. Her reputation and lifestyle intrigues me, so mysterious," Jesse mused.

Putting the final touch on Jesse's foot massage, Voula asked, "Are you hungry? I made some of the muesli bread you like, and I could use a cup of coffee."

"You don't have to wait on me Voula, I can get it."

"It's no bother, want some of that honey on your toast?"

"Yes please, I can't believe the beautiful honey on this island, must have enchanted bees. I don't think I'll ever touch sugar again. That one I just bought, I swear tastes of cinnamon, how's that?"

"The bees probably pollinated a carnation field, you know the little wild ones called 'pinks,' not for their color though, the red ones especially smell of cinnamon. Pick one and smell next time you go for a walk."

Voula brought out a tray and set it on the terrace table, Jesse pulled-up a chair, as she poured their coffees.

"Are you working tonight, Jess?"

"Yep, and every night until next Monday. The devil doesn't take weekends off," Jesse said, biting into her toast. "Mm, so good, your bread's like nutty, crunchy porridge, but way better." She licked the honey from her fingers.

"Glad you like it… Jess, how with all the late hours you'll be working can you do the watercolor workshops?"

"Can't, that's why I've changed my plans. It's okay though, with what this job pays me, I won't need that chump change. But I do want to take that Admiral Banfield up on his offer of a commission for his family's portrait. In fact, I'm going to try to see him today."

"Banfield lives in Kassiopi, doesn't he?"

"Rear Admiral, retired, if you please, and likely loaded. Remind me, where's Kassiopi?" Jesse said.

"The North-east tip of the island, they call it Kensington-on Sea, because so many rich Brits and Russian oligarchs have villas there or anchor their yachts for the season. I hear from my connections at the market, his family's been a Corfiot fixture for generations and his wife's well-connected too, comes from a titled, diplomatic family, has high friends in the British government and Foreign Office."

"Wow, you're not so badly connected yourself, Voula!" Jesse exclaimed, pouring them more coffee.

"If you want to know what really goes on, ask the cleaning ladies, the cooks and gardeners, the market vendors, they are the eyes and ears of every community. But what about you? I need some real 'girlfriend goss'…how's hunky Peter, with the 'bedroom eyes' treating you?"

"Oh, so you noticed, eh?"

"Course I noticed, I may be old, but I'm not dead!"

"Voula, you're not old. And as for how Peter treats me, he makes me feel like a princess, but also, like an equal. He gets me to push my boundaries, I like that. It's what I need right now."

"Unlike safe, secure Josh who knows exactly what you want, and how your lives should go?"

"Yes. Being here, working at a completely inappropriate job for my qualifications, being with whom appears a completely inappropriate man, is just what I need. I can suddenly breathe!

"For the last few years, I've held my breath in

anticipation of my profs' judgement, my parents' judgement, my friends' judgement. I never exhaled, took a beat, to check my feelings about happiness. Now I think, it's my judgement of what's happiness for me that counts," Jesse said, emphatically, getting-up to clear the table.

"I suppose you're right, Jess. At the end of the day, only we'll answer for our lives and how we've lived them."

"I know, I'm a big girl."

"Yes, you are, just don't forget that if you need to, you can always talk to me, without judgement."

"I'll remember that, thanks. You know Voula, my mom doesn't approve of you, but she didn't really give you a chance. You're a cool lady, I'm glad you and nonno are together," Jesse said, giving her a little hug, before exiting.

Well, thought Voula, *that's an unexpected turn. But lines of communication are open, and I think we're going to need them.*

JESSE PUT DOWN the kickstand on her yellow Vespa, removed her helmet, and shook her long, auburn curls loose. She regarded the handsome Palladian portico and double staircase fronting the Banfield's brilliant white villa. *So, this is how the other half of Corfu live.* It reminded her of a place she saw in Padua, on a high school Art trip to Italy. She recalled fantasizing how fabulous it would be to live in a place like that; perfectly, classically symmetrical, so civilized, and sophisticated. Now, she was about to find out how that privilege dwelt. The Admiral must've been watching for her, as he appeared in the doorway before she reached it.

"So, you found us alright, did you?" he said smiling, extending his hand, looking more like the gardener than a Rear-Admiral, relaxed in his faded, blue-striped jersey, shabby chinos, and battered espadrilles. His wavy, surprisingly full head of silver hair curling up on his collar.

"Yes, perfectly alright, thank-you. Actually, you're hard to miss, having the highest vantage point on the hill," she shook his hand, then turned, to admire the view, "Lovely, just lovely, the wonderful aspect you have here, overlooking the sea, in the near distance, Albania, isn't it? Nice breeze too. You certainly don't need a.c. up here."

"Perish the thought! An abomination, air conditioning, never had it in Nairobu or Bengal, you know. Must just adjust to local conditions, and the way of life, 'Only mad dogs and Englishmen, go out in the noon day sun', I'm afraid. It's the reason my very sensible Greek forbears built on the windward side of the island," he smiled.

"So, you're a native?"

"On mater's side, great grandmama founded the family fortune on her back. Widowed three times; an Earl, a member of parliament, and the last husband, first cousin of Greece's King George the first, grandfather of the Duke of Edinburgh."

He led her through to the elegantly appointed drawing room where his wife waited with their three grandchildren. The admiral made his introductions, "Claudia, this is Jesse Ponti, the young artist I told you about."

The tall, tanned, slender brunette rose to take her hand, "Hello! So nice to meet you, you brave young thing. Think you can get these three to stay still for more than five minutes?" She pointed to her two grandsons, who were wrestling over their belea-guered Irish setter, while their little sister practiced hitting a ping-pong ball against the silk couch cushions.

"Can we go out to play soon, grandma? It's so boring inside."

"Not yet, Emma, now use your manners please, and say hello to Jesse,"

"Hello Jesse", the seven-year-old said, without taking her eye off her ball.

"Hello, Emma. And you two gentlemen are?" Jesse asked the two boys.

"How'd you do, I'm Archie", said the twelve-year-old, jumping-up to shake her hand. "And this is my younger brother, the feral, Myles. Stand-up Myles, and greet the lady, will you?"

The nine-year-old rose reluctantly, pushed his long bangs out of his eyes and extended a grubby hand, "Hello."

"Hello, Myles, pleased to meet you," Jesse said, shaking his fingers, avoiding his dirty palm.

Jesse took a moment to survey the assembled Banfields. She judged them to be an attractive, quintessentially English-looking family, with their fair, ruddy complexions, flaxen hair, bright blue eyes and pink, bow-lips, an unmistakable, generational trait, looks clearly inherited from the admiral. They almost looked too typical. The exception was Claudia.

Mrs. Banfield looked to be about twenty years younger than her octogenarian husband, and held herself with a gracious, almost continental air. Her dyed up-swept bob, large, dark, wide-set eyes and lithe physique were reminiscent of Jackie 'O', as was her casually chic attire; form-fitting white capris and a blue silk jersey, with a red paisley neckerchief, little make-up, minimal jewelry, white-opal studs, diamond wedding rings and a sleek, silver Movado.

Hmm, definitely the second wife, thought Jesse.

"Please, can we go swimming now? It's been a good hour since lunch, so we won't get cramp," Myles pleaded, Emma joined-in, "Yes please, please, grandma, I'm boiling, *and* I'm bored!" she pouted.

"Oh dear, heaven forbid!" the Admiral mocked. "Well old girl, shall we ask Janita to get them changed and in the pool before all hell breaks loose?"

"Sounds like a plan, then we can have a quiet, sensible talk with Jesse, and perhaps a cocktail on the patio? We haven't offered her any hospitality. She must think we're barbarians," Claudia smiled at Jesse. "Would you like a Pimm's?"

"Sure, thanks," Jesse replied, having no idea what a 'Pimm's' was.

"Coming-up," said the Admiral.

The nanny, Janita, was summoned and the noisy brood herded to the cabana and pool. Claudia led Jesse out to the terrace overlooking their handsome parterre, with its fragrant rosemary hedges, precision-clipped, geometric boxwood edging, surrounding pleasing arrangements of various flowering plants, and topiary shrubs. The palette was mostly pastels, unified with lots of white.

"Oh, this is beautiful, Claudia. Who designed your gardens?" Jesse asked.

"I did. I love garden design, it's my creative outlet. Do you know about it, Jesse?"

"A little. But no, not much really."

"I was inspired by Sissinghurst, the gardens of Vita Sackville-West. You know, the woman Woolf's, *Orlando* was based-on?"

Jesse didn't, but nodded, implying that she did, then observed, "This garden isn't typical for here, where you see people choose mostly hot colors and tropicals," thinking especially of the exuberant colors in Voula's plantings.

"I know, but the admiral and I often entertain out here in the evenings, even when it's just us two, we're night owls, and sit out until past midnight. The evenings being cool, the night skies so clear, and full of stars…magnificent.

"That's when a white garden really, literally shines, whereas deep saturated colors disappear. At night, all the pale pastels and the whites glow. It's magic! In bright daylight, I'm afraid they're rather washed-out. You must come when next we have a dinner party, and see what I mean." Claudia's expression was animated, her eyes lighting-up thinking of the enchantment of her brilliant, moonlit garden.

"Thank-you, that'd be lovely." Jesse said, thinking such an invitation might also yield her a few more lucrative commissions.

"Here we are ladies," the Admiral announced as he put down the heavy silver tray of drinks.

"Oh, thank-you darling. Lemon for me please," Claudia said, as the Admiral picked-up small silver tongs to add a few slices to his wife's drink.

"And you, Jesse, orange, lemon, lime, or without?" he asked.

"Orange slice, please."

The admiral served his guest, then settled himself into his chair, lifted his cut-glass tumbler and said, 'Cheers!"

"Cheers," the ladies replied, taking a long, appreciative sip.

"This is so refreshing," said Jesse, "I've never had this Pimm's before. I really like the slight tang of ginger, it's nice with the orange." She took another sip.

"Reed's Jamaican ginger ale, dash of bitters, Pimm's Number1 cup and chipped ice, that's key," said the Admiral, clearly enjoying his cocktail.

Jesse pulled-out her phone, scrolling through her gallery, she offered it to Claudia, "Would you like to see some of my work? I confess, I only have about six portraits, but they're representative of my current approach."

"Oh, thank-you. Yes, very nice indeed. But I have seen your work over the bar in the Asteri, and that's good enough for me. I like the Impressionist palette and brushwork; I think it flatters the subject. It'll work well with our other pieces; I've inherited a Boudin, a minor, dull Pissaro, an early Dali, from his developmental period, and for figures, a rather dour, Winslow Homer etching, then there's a small group study by Berthe Morisot, and a sweet, genre scene by Mary Cassat…"

"Stop showing-off old girl. I bought a couple of Mikhail Larionov's landscapes in the seventies. And for our silver anniversary, didn't I present you with a Tissot?" the admiral countered, satisfied with himself.

"Yes, darling you did. It's the jewel in the crown, my favorite piece. A portrait of his mistress, Kathleen Newton, and her two little boys in their garden in St. John's Wood."

The admiral was quick to add, "We don't keep them all here of course, here's only copies of things we admire, our real stuff's stored in the pied-a-terre in Blighty. In any case, I'm glad you don't follow hideous Lucien Freud, or even worse, that horror, Francis Bacon!" he spat out, in disgust.

"Oh well, I'm afraid I admire Freud's portraiture, and am really moved by Bacon's work," Jesse countered, unwilling to betray her sincere opinion.

"Of course, you are dear!" Claudia said, topping-up their drinks from the pitcher. "You're an artist. We're just dotty old collectors. It's right you should be interested in work that pushes the boundaries of patrons' tastes and the public's expectations.

"Now, I love avant-garde landscape design, wanted to paint the olive and lemon trees we lost one terrible winter, a Mediterranean blue and deep red coral, as kind of sculptural pieces punctuating the grove; I'd seen it done in Garden Design one issue, but the admiral said it'd be daft. So, I relented and planted new ones instead. But then I'm not an artist, or I wouldn't have compromised," she smiled.

Jesse was warming to her hostess, finding her charming, witty, and intelligent. "Let's talk about what you envision for your family portrait," Jesse said, wanting to steer the discourse towards the project.

The admiral was eager to offer his opinion, "What d'ya think of the group assembled in the great room, her ladyship seated, adoring husband behind, hands on shoulders, various little Banfields framing us, loyal setter at their feet, French doors in background, suggestion of gardens beyond. Kids in school blazers, Bermuda shorts and a little kilt for Emma?"

Both women stared at him, Claudia declared, "Oh, how dull, Harry! No, no. Let's do a 'plein air' portrait, me seated on the white wrought iron settee by the lily pond, boys lolling, as they may, in the foreground, on the grass, loyal setter between them, god knows she deserves her moment. Perhaps little Emma reclining on my lap, with her scruffy, stuffed unicorn.

"I have a long full skirt with a pretty poppy print, that'd be a nice focus, show it to you afterwards? The admiral can stand behind me, in his yachting whites, braid cap on, jaunty angle, telescope tucked beneath an arm?"

"Sounds more like it, playful, like your family. The children should be at ease, I don't like stiff poses, especially not for kids."

When they finished their drinks, they took Jesse down to the lily pond, to see the setting, which she judged as idyllic, especially with the ancient willow as a backdrop, Cassatt herself could do no better.

Claudia went to check on the children, leaving the admiral and Jesse to discuss price, and other practical matters. Jesse agreed to return in two weeks, during time-off, to sketch and take photographs to work from in the studio she would set-up in the spare bedroom.

AFTER MUCH WALKING and ruminating around the abandoned monastery of Agioi Deka, mountain of 'The Ten Saints' on the south-west range, where when he could drive no further, Aldo abandoned his car and set out on foot on a network of ancient, cobbled mule paths which eventually led to the summit and the ruin. A tiring descent he was now dreading, hoping he could avoid a circuitous route.

Perhaps it was his constant angrily muttered curses to the saints, or just his good sense of direction that led him fairly directly back to the car. He now had a firm plan and a terrible thirst, which he would quench in the eponymous village tucked into the south slope of the mountain.

Aldo ordered a small beer at the bar, as the waiter poured, he took out Matt's card and phoned his number. He didn't know why, but he was surprised when Matt answered immediately. It unnerved him, as if he was, just at that moment, waiting for his call. As it happened, he was in town and could meet Aldo at the taverna in about thirty minutes.

Ordering a second beer and some mezes, he

texted Voula his apologies, said he wouldn't be back until late afternoon, as compensation, he'd take her to The Venetian Well for dinner, one of the best Italian restaurants in Corfu Town. She returned a terse text, accepting the offer, noting that she'd be back late too, as she decided not to wait on him, but to get her hair done and do some shopping instead. He breathed a sigh of relief. Now, all he needed was to negotiate a deal with Matt Olivera, and his criminal web.

He decided it was better to go to the enemy, than wait in defiant anticipation, for them to come and lean on him, putting Aldo in a desperate and weak position. No, it was better to negotiate on an equal footing with Matt, put forth his own plan, quietly gather evidence, look for a weakness to exploit, get the upper hand, then disentangle himself. But it would take time and patience.

"Well, this is a nice out-of-the-way spot, Aldo. Beer please, lager, and make it a long one," Matt said as he mounted the bar stool next to his companion.

"Isn't it though. Nice views from the summit if you like hiking."

"Thanks, I'll check it out some time, always interested in exploring remote spots," Matt gave him an oily grin, raised his glass, and drank deeply.

Waiting for Matt to quench his thirst, Aldo dove

in, "I have a proposition for you paesan, been thinking about your interest in investing in my enterprise. I think to start, we be discreet, set-up a company, call it Star Catering, you register as president, I'll be operations manager, the rest of your friends, designated as you see fit."

"What about your friends, Aldo, where do they come in?"

"They don't. Why should I cut them in? They're only silent partners, I do all the heavy-lifting around here, why shouldn't I have a private pension plan, like you, eh?"

"Why not indeed, a little greedy though, Aldo," Matt said thoughtfully, not liking this twist, wanting Aldo with more 'skin in the game', with a view to he and Peter, eventually squeezing them out, taking-over the real estate.

"*Poco a poco*, little by little paesan. Like I said, begin discreetly, later I can either buy some of them out, or bring them around. In the meantime, there's laundry to do, right? So, we can wash a lot of sheets every month through the company, getting goods from your 'suppliers', which you then sell-on at a tidy profit," Aldo ordered another beer, trying hard to stay calm, look casual and seem clever.

"Uh-huh," Matt uttered, rubbing his chin. He took another sip of beer, then fiddled with his beer mat, hoping to wind Aldo up. Finally, he spoke, turning to face his companion, said, "Tell you how this is going to go down. We set-up that company, sure, but your girlfriend, Voula, is it? From Ukraine, if I'm not mistaken?"

"What she got to do with it?"

"She's our president, silent, of course. Get her documents, and we'll register the joint stocks in Ukraine. I'll take care of the rest of the board, docs, names etc. Now, we'll bill for catering, monthly as you say and product. Then you take it out the back door here, I get my cut, you and your people get yours. Got it?"

This was going badly. Aldo fought hard to stay on the bar stool and not show his fury, "But how and where am I going to move this product without anyone knowing?"

"Your problem, as vice-president of sales and distribution, paesan."

"And what about Voula? She won't want any part of this. If she finds out, she may just take-off. Then, I won't be able to control what she'll do, or say," Aldo hoped this would give Matt pause.

"Voula? She doesn't need to know about our business, or her new promotion. Please don't tell me you've become that soft, you can't handle a woman? 'Cause if you can't, I will. Just get those documents for me by tomorrow, meet me in the morning, at that abandoned monastery, at ten."

Matt stood, clapped Aldo on the back, and left chuckling, shaking his head.

Aldo sat for a minute, frozen, staring ahead, afraid to move as his stomach was churning, small beads of sweat broke-out on his forehead. *Shit! What have I done? He's got me and Voula now. Think, think, I need time to think.* But time, for Aldo, for now, had run out.

HEY, BIG TIPPER

THE GEMINI HAIR salon and spa, by the ancient Venetian Fort, was Voula's go-to place for pampering. As she leafed through a hair design magazine, ensconced in a comfy auto-massage treatment chair, Voula tried to let go of her frustration with Aldo's moodiness, and just look forward to a nice dinner out with him.

Melina, the owner and Voula's stylist, busy touching-up her roots, asked, "So, do you want the same look? A little trim and some shaping, then a blow-out? Maybe some twist curls, along the bottom, or I could take it right-up to the crown...just for more height and bounce, nice and youthful?

Voula thought a moment, "No, Melina. Let's do something different this time. I need a change, like this, nice and short," she held-up the magazine.

"Melina took a close look at the pictures, front, back and sides of a short, layered bob with long, sexy, sideswept feathered bangs, covering the ears, but short and layered at the back. "Yes! I like this look for you, perfect! It accents your eyes and is playful. Your hair is just long enough to work with too. Can wear it combed back. It's a good cut, very versatile, easy to maintain," she said, smiling, putting the last of the dye on Voula's roots, then setting the timer.

"I'll be back, want a tea or coffee before I go?"

"No thanks, Melina. Nicky's going to give me a manicure…and here she is!"

"Hi Voula, good to see you," Nicky said, swivelling the treatment chair around to face her, installing the tray-stand. She took Voula's hands in hers and inspected her nails, "Oh my, and what have you been up to? These are in rough shape, lady!"

"I know. I forget the gardening gloves, and the rubber gloves for chores. All those years as a professional cleaner, you'd think I'd know better," Voula said, regarding her red knuckles, broken, discoloured nails and ragged cuticles.

"Never mind, I'll fix. I've got some gorgeous whipped almond oil and honey butter. Soothing and hydrating, made here on the island. But first, lets get these hands into some warm, spa-water, soften them up. She plunged Voula's hands into the spa bath and turned it on.

While it bubbled away, Nicky said, "You know the last tarot reading you did for me was spot-on. George *was* seeing his ex, the scumbag. Anyway, I don't care, I've moved on. I'm seeing his younger, richer cousin, Spiros.

"Who, unlike Mr. Scumbag, has no baggage. Never been married, no kids. And the extra bonus is, George has always been jealous of him!" Nicky laughed, lifting Voula's hands out of the water, drying them off, then massaging-in a generous slathering of cream.

"Well, I'm glad it turned out for you. Now, if I can only sort out my own man problems," Voula sighed.

"Oh, what's the issue? What's the tarot say about it?"

"The issue is, I think Aldo is worried about something, or more to the point, someone, from his past. Tarot says, something sinister is lurking there. Goes off on his own for long walks, is very secretive."

"Oh no, don't tell me an ex, maybe with a secret

family? Is she coming here?" Nicky's voice rose, her eyes widened with excitement, as she took-in a quick, audible breath.

"No, no. It's nothing like that. Don't let that Pisces imagination run away with you. It's just a guy who showed-up at the taverna, bit creepy, from Aldo's hometown.

"He works for that Medusa on her yacht, hired Jesse to do some hostessing. I don't like him, but Aldo *really* doesn't like him, and for reasons he won't divulge, or just soft-pedals."

"So, no ex and hidden family then?"

"Sorry to disappoint, Nicky, but no hidden family," Voula chuckled.

"Hmm, but I know what you mean about that Medusa crew, a few of them have come in here, they're big tippers, but on a few occasions, I could swear they were high. And the Gorgon herself came in last week."

"High? What do you mean, high?"

"Well, dilated pupils. I know, I did their lashes, and very kinda 'dreamy' but hyper too, laughing and giggling too much. They also brought in some champagne and wanted to have it during their treatments. I said, no, but Melina told them okay, but just this once. In future, if they wanted to book the place for a spa party, with catering, it could be arranged."

"Uh-huh, and what about the Gorgon?" Voula asked with interest.

"La Medusa? Good looking, in great shape. Hard to tell age, maybe early forties. Very Eastern European looking, deep-set, slanted eyes, high cheekbones.

Melina walked over to add, "Cool and demanding. We treated her in our private room. Some waxing, laser therapy, fillers, said very little, was on her phone a lot, yammering away in Russian, or something like that, brusque. But again, good tipper. Bought lots of the almond oil butter too."

"Was she alone?"

"Yes and no." Melina wet on, "A big, heavy-looking guy, escorted her in, then waited outside in her car. When she was finished, he came in and escorted her out. That was it."

"A bit weird, he seemed like a bodyguard, but why she needs a bodyguard to go to a salon in quiet, little Corfu is beyond me. What a prima donna!' Nicky scoffed.

WHEN HER HAIR was cut and her nails French-polished, Voula, paid her bill saying, "Thanks, ladies. I feel like a new woman, and I'm really loving this cut." She admired herself in the mirror, playing with her bangs.

"It looks great on you, good choice. I just hope Aldo has somewhere to take all this gorgeousness," Melina said, with a sweeping gesture towards her client.

"We're going to the Venetian Well tonight." Then checking the time, Voula said, "But looks like I have a couple more hours to kill."

"Why don't you go to Kassiopi then, Celeste Boutique has a mid-season sale, they have some really pretty lines in this summer."

"Okay, think I will. New hairdo, cries-out for new dress. Thanks, Melina," Voula said, as she turned to go.

"I'll text Celeste, tell her you're coming. She's my best friend, will give you a little something extra," Melina winked at her favourite client.

THE BOUTIQUE'S SALE did not disappoint, neither did the service she got from Celeste, who threw in a pretty, floral wrist band to complement the lavender, full-length silk jersey shift and long, chiffon, hibiscus-motif scarf Voula decided she couldn't live without.

She was surprised how good she looked in the form-fitting dress, having lost fifteen pounds without really trying, just walking more, eating lots of fish, and helping out at the Asteri. Voula didn't believe in restrictive diets, she just ate what was best from the land she found herself in, that and hard work, would do it. And after a hard day's work of self-care, she decided it was time for a little white wine spritzer at a nearby café before she headed home.

Leaning back in her chair facing the sun-lit square, she put on her dark glasses and took a sip of her cool drink, *mm, that's nice, what a good day, I'm glad Aldo stood me up. I needed this 'me time', but I won't tell him that,* she laughed inwardly. It was then she noticed a man at the adjacent table, smiling at her. She wondered if she'd been muttering aloud to herself…*probably thinks I'm nuts…hmm, stocky, moon-face, white socks with sandals, expensive watch, German or Eastern European?* she smiled back and raised her glass, he copied her gesture.

Just when she thought he might come over for a chat, and perhaps another spritzer, a second man appeared. Tall, well-built, high cheekbones, broken nose, granite jaw, slightly slanted eyes, thick, gold chains, *this one, definitely Cossack,* she shuddered, remembering the repressive, Soviet regime plaguing her young life in Ukraine.

The man sat down, ordered a vodka and began firing-off orders in Russian at what Voula could only imagine was a cringing 'peon', at the other end of the phone. She understood Russian fairly well, having been made to study it at school under the Soviets, then pursuing fluency in hopes of securing a government job, that was all before 'the fall', of course. Voula wished she was sat closer to them; she felt intrigued for some reason and wanted to know more about them. *They didn't seem to be here for pleasure, so what business would two Russians be doing in Corfu?* she wondered.

Voula didn't need to wonder long, as the Cossack, after quickly downing two shots of vodka, seemed all about business. He was demanding information from the second man, a kind of report of who was coming and going, and when...*sounds like, from Medina? No, not Medina, Medusa! ...Why are these two watching the Medusa?*

The Cossack suddenly looked in her direction, sensing her interest, she quickly looked down at her purse, pretending to rummage around for a tissue, *stupid! just don't take out your phone...he'll think you're watching him...got it...*she felt her phone in the bag and turned it off, without taking it out, she didn't want to have to speak, or they would hear she was Eastern European, and likely clam-up.

Voula made, nonchalantly, to adjust her sandal strap, seeming not to notice the penetrating gaze of the Cossack and his friend, in what was an otherwise empty patio. Just then, the young waiter asked her if she wanted another drink, she nodded and smiled, 'yes'.

She needed the ladies' room but crossed her legs, determined to sit out their exchange, *damn, if only I had a magazine or something…ah! Yes! Thank-you Celeste!* Voula smiled as she reached into her glossy, boutique bag to extract a copy of one of their lines' fall catalogue. Pretending to be engrossed in the slim publication, while she waited for her drink order, Voula prayed they'd stay longer and say more.

The men seemed to relax and resume their exchange…even though their voices were lowered now, she could just make out a few phrases, the Cossack was talking about shipments, from boats, on boats…some going to…Crow's Nest? Then Deutsche Bank in Berlin? None of this made sense to Voula, which was just as well, as the men rose abruptly, threw some money on the table and left, the Cossack giving her 'the fisheye' on his way out.

She pretended not to notice their departure for a few minutes, when she judged it safe to go to the bar, settle her tab, and make a few discreet inquiries.

Making a point of offering a generous tip to her server, she smiled warmly and asked, "Those two men, just here, where do they stay? I only ask because I work in a taverna in Gouvia, and we've seen a few more Russian tourists lately too…" she trailed-off hoping this kid was talkative or bored enough to pick-up her thread and gossip.

"Those guys, they stay on those big boats, anchor near Kassiopi, you know, little Kensington…they have the big, luxury yachts, porn stars and bankers, and lots of…" he made a deep nasal, sniffing noise, grabbed his crotch, laughed, and nodded.

"Oh? Gotcha! Well, there goes the neighborhood, eh. I hope they're good tippers," Voula smiled, waving goodbye, dying to get home.

AFTER A QUIET, sumptuous, and satisfying dinner at The Venetian Well, followed by a moonlit walk around the Old Town, and a visit to the Asteri for a night cap and to pick-up that day's earnings, Aldo and Voula were ready for sleep. Voula turned-down the duvet on her side of the old hand-carved wooden bed, and clambered in. Aldo's slow, quiet breathing signalled he was close to being asleep.

He opened one eye and peered at her, "You

looked lovely tonight."

"Yes, so you told me earlier, but that's okay, I can hear it again."

"You enjoy the risotto? Mine was a bit salty."

"I liked it, the grilled branzino too. I noticed you didn't eat much though, you were very quiet, something on your mind?" she asked softly.

"No, nothing more than I already said. My walk didn't help, I've no idea how to get Jesse away from that crowd, I have no proof, just instinct. And she isn't going to quit her lucrative, glamorous job 'cause of my instinct, is she?" Aldo was fully awake now, both eyes open.

"No. But your instinct is good, if what I heard at the hair studio is right, those kids are partiers, into drugs."

"Drugs? What kind of drugs?" he said, sitting up.

"Well, not heroin, but likely pot, maybe cocaine? Do you think Jess would try that stuff?"

"No…. Who knows? Maybe she already has? So hard to know these days. She's not much of a partier, she was always serious, studious. I can't see her being influenced into drug use, Jess's too tough-minded."

"I think you're right. But still, we have to keep our eyes and ears open, right?"

"Right," he yawned. "God, I'm tired… I did put the takings in the safe tonight, didn't I?"

"Yes, first thing when we came in. You're getting senile, old man," she chuckled.

"And all of our documents are in there too, right?"

"Of course. Why do you ask?"

"I just want to make sure everything's safely locked away, Nikos told me there's been a spate of break-ins lately. That's all."

"Break-ins? Where? I haven't heard of any," Voula said, a little suspicious.

"In his neighborhood, probably just two and he's hysterical, you know how he exaggerates. Anyway, I'll take the deposit and our documents to the bank tomorrow morning, I want to see the manager about some of the fees they're charging us, you sleep in. I may just go directly to the Asteri afterwards, so I won't see you until later, okay?"

"Okay. Is there anything else I should know?"

"Anything else? No, there's nothing you should know. Now, let's get some sleep."

Voula stayed awake for awhile after Aldo began to snore. Wondering how to get at what he was hiding, she knew there was something, but confrontation, accusations and angry words wouldn't get her any closer to the truth.

Chapter Four

SATAN'S ALGORITHM

TWO WEEKS LATER, Jesse and Wu Tang were having their break in the staff lounge, when Jesse observed how exceptionally well the high rollers at the blackjack tables were doing that night:

"They winning a lot? Ha! That don't bother la Medusa, she's the house, in the long play, house always wins. Jesse, winning is just Satan's way of keepin' you losin'… he's got his algorithm straight, knows just when to give you that little hit of adrenalin, when to let you crash and burn. Think, 'I did it once, I can do it again'," Wu tang exclaimed.

"Why don't we ever see la Medusa down here on the floor, gambling with the guests?" Jesse asked.

"Ha! Ha! …la Medusa? Oh no, child, she's no gambler, she's the house, likes herself a sure thing, knows never to get high on her own supply. She gives credit to high rollers, watching them become high losers, then they payback in many ways, more than they bargained for." He laughed a hearty belly laugh, his huge biceps flexing over his muscular stomach, his gold teeth flashing in delight, at his own witty wisdom.

Just then, Peter burst into the staff lounge, looking a little sweaty and tense, "Hello, my lovely," he said, seeing Jesse, then grabbed Wu Tang playfully, by the lapels, "Wu, where's my blow man? Don't tell me you two dipped-in already with out me!"

"Get back bro, don't fondle the merchandise, and I ain't your lovely!" Wu Tang laughed, taking a packet, and three straws from his vest pocket.

"Well line 'er up, man, I'm gasping. That floor's hopping tonight, must be the full moon," Peter said rubbing his hands together.

Jesse stood by, incredulous at what she knew was happening, "What? Are you nuts? Guys, what if you get caught, la Medusa will kill you!"

"La Medusa? I don't think so," Peter said, handing her a straw.

"No, thanks. I'm not into that. Anyway, how do you know one of the punters out there isn't an undercover narc?"

"There is, but he be paid him his share, already!" Wu Tang laughed, after snorting-up a generous line of cocaine, and watching Peter do his, before going in for half of Jesse's.

Peter stood back, let out a sigh of relief, smiled

and asked Jesse, "You sure? Gonna be a long night, and this helps you chill and keep up too. C'mon, a little taste won't hurt you," Peter pleaded, as Jesse moved closer to the door.

"Look, just go like this, like cleaning your teeth, only better!" he laughed picking-up a little of the white powder on his index finger and rubbing it on his gums.

"My break is over. I'm going back out," Jesse said coldly, slamming the door behind her.

Hitting the floor, feeling tense and angry, Jesse ignored Charlie and Suze on their way to the lounge, dancing, 'raising the roof', chanting softly, "This is how we do it, This is how we do it."

Yes, Jesse thought, *it's going to be a very long night.*

It was three a.m., when Matt finally took her home, she was tired, chilled and had a thumping headache, she didn't want to talk to him, but he kept yammering away.

"You seem out of sorts, Jess. Are you okay? If you're coming down with something, I'm sure I can arrange some sick time off for you," he said, too solicitously.

"No, thanks."

"Okay…well then, what's bugging you? You can talk to your uncle Matt. I'm not nearly as scary as the kids make out," he said, turning to give her a wolfish smile.

"I'm fine, thanks."

"Is it Aldo? Is he giving you grief? He doesn't understand the young, like I do. I know he can be a real stick in the mud, a party-pooper, always was," Matt sighed, shaking his head.

"My nonno's a wonderful person, hard working, my best friend when I was a kid. So, tell me Matt, just why do you think you have such a 'connection' to us younger folk, eh?" Jesse asked a little belligerently.

"Oh now, Jess, relax. I didn't mean to throw shade on Aldo, sure, he's a real family man. I just meant that sometimes he can be a little 'Mr. Straight and Narrow', emphasis on straight."

"What do you mean 'emphasis on straight'?"

"Well, he would be, wouldn't he? I mean given his background," Matt pulled back on the throttle, slowing the noisy engines, so they could talk properly.

"What's all this inuendo about my grandfather, just spit it out, whatever you have to say, 'cause I'm really getting fed-up right now!" Jesse surprised herself and Matt with her impatient, forthright command.

"Well," he said, calmly, "your nonno took a lot of

abuse from his alcoholic father, is all I'm saying, and so doesn't like drunkenness, or drugs. Sorry, I thought you knew."

"Course I knew," Jesse lied, pulling her jacket tightly around her. "My family's business, is just that, our business. Maybe you should 'straighten out' your own family."

Matt was becoming annoyed at the audacity of this young woman, one whom he thought he could charm and manipulate. "My family? Now who's using innuendos?" he asked as he pulled-up close enough to her dock, for Jesse risking climbing-out of the tender, not waiting for Matt to disembark first and tie it up.

She looked down at him from the dock and shouted, "I mean Peter and the others are snorting cocaine, and if you don't stop it, I'm not coming back!" with that she ran off towards the house, leaving an angry and vengeful Matt to get back and sever some heads.

THE NEXT DAY, Peter's chastened friends appeared on deck early, waiting for Matt's instructions for the day. Any possibility of shore leave had been revoked and last night's tips had been withheld as punishment for their indiscretion. The only exception to shore leave was Peter, who was despatched to make amends with Jesse and try to get her back within the fold. After getting their orders, they sullenly went about the day, as they watched with envy, Peter's escape to the mainland.

For the third time, Peter knocked hard on the back door, he was sure Jess was there, having waited by the marina road exit, for Aldo's car to leave bearing he and Voula. Jess' Vespa was there, so she must be home, he was fairly sure she couldn't see the back door, *so why wasn't she answering?*

"What?…Oh, it's *you*," Jesse said, yanking the door open, initially annoyed at the loud knocking, then disappointed at the visitor.

"Handy man, ma'am," Peter responded, holding-up a toolbox, smiling his brightest smile.

"Handy man? I didn't order any 'handy man', get lost," she said, going to slam the door closed, when he put out his hand to stop it.

"I'm here to fix the broken shutters that you complained about. The ones that interrupt your beauty sleep, not that you need it, being as beautiful as you are…'

Jesse, rolling her eyes, interrupted with, "Oh, puhleeze!"

"Nonetheless," Peter continued, undaunted, "seeing as no one else is here to remedy your dilemma, I volunteer. "I'll just do that, as a goodwill gesture, and 'cause I love you to bits, then be on my way, okay?" he said, still smiling, his dazzling smile.

Jesse quickly noted the 'love you to bits' part, and took-in that smile, and the fact that she really wanted the shutters repaired, so relented, and showed her unbidden visitor upstairs to her bedroom.

"Here they are. See, most of the slats are hanging off the frames, and the frames are off the hinges," she pointed to the sad stack of broken shutters piled in the corner of the room.

"Uh-huh," Peter said, thoughtfully as he picked one up and played around with the slats, inspected the frame and hinges. "Well, the good news is, there's no rot, the hardware is in fairly decent, if a little rusty shape, so we can definitely repair with what's here. The patient will live to see a full and happy life, giving you shade when you need it, a barrier from the wind and rain etc." he said happily, looking to Jesse for her reaction.

"Good, fine. So, where will you work and how long will you take?" she asked arms folded, not wanting to seem approachable or even grateful.

"Downstairs, out the back, I noticed there were a couple of sawhorses there, perfect to work on. Now, if you'll just give me a hand taking these downstairs,

I'll be out in no time," he said confidently, picking-up a couple of shutters, making for the door.

Jesse picked-up the remaining two, and following him asked, "Don't you need an electric outlet?"

"No, all those power tools are battery, fully-charged and rarin' to go."

"Good, then you won't need anything else?" Jesse said, as she put down her load.

"Nope, maybe a cold beer at noon? Just to keep hydrated," Peter said, squinting at the sun, now nearly at its highest in the sky.

"I'll see," Jesse said, tersely, going back inside to her makeshift studio, to resume work on her commission for the Banfields. She was in the process of laying down the underpainting in the figures she'd blocked-in earlier, but sorting through her reference photographs, pondering what the overall palette should be, 'cool or warm' – she found she just couldn't concentrate.

Peter's turning-up had unsettled her, she had almost expected it, but not his cheerful demeanor. Jesse had expected anger from him, maybe contrition, but not this happy-go-lucky, 'nothing's wrong' attitude. It was as if the incident hadn't happened. The more she thought about it, the more she felt indignant at his emotional ambush, catching her off-guard, making her an offer, he knew she wouldn't refuse, but not offering an apology. She felt herself becoming more indignant by the minute, *Well, that's not good enough, I'm having it out with him right now!*

A worked-up Jesse ran down the stairs to the back, where Peter was screwing some slats onto a frame, and surprised him shouting, "Hey! What do you think, that I'm an idiot? You can try to push drugs on me one minute, then turn up here, all smiles and help, and expect me to forget what an asshole you are?"

Peter dropped the drill, and turned to face his accuser, "Asshole? I'm trying to help you out here and make amends. I'm sorry, I just thought you'd know that."

"Why would I assume that, when you haven't even addressed the issue, or apologized?" Jesse said, hands on her hips.

"I am apologizing, this is me, apologizing. Okay…I'm sorry that I offered you drugs." Peter said, nonchalantly.

"What? Like, that's it? What about *your* drug use? What about the fact that you got me involved in employment where drugs were being used? I don't want to end-up in a Greek prison, *you idiot!*" Jesse was screaming now and awfully close to ordering him off the property.

Peter stepped towards her, placing a hand on her arm, "Calm down, it'll never happen again. I will never offer you drugs, or take drugs again," he said, shaking her a little, "and after Matt's reprimand today, I very much doubt if the others will either." He placed both hands on her shoulders and looked directly into her eyes.

Jesse stood silent for a moment, her anger subsiding, her pulse slowing down. She cared a lot about Peter, was infatuated with him, he had a hold over her that she wasn't entirely comfortable with. Jesse dropped her arms, accepting his embrace, sobbing a little, as he reassured her.

"Okay, I believe you, but please, never lie to me, or compromise me again," she said softly, into his warm neck.

"No, never, never again, I swear," Peter replied, stroking her hair, then kissing her. "Now, leave me alone to finish these, I want to get them up for you before I have to head back. Will you come to work tonight?"

Jesse thought a moment. "Yes, I will," adding as she turned to go, "if you want, I can make us some lunch."

"Sure, that'd be great, thanks."

"Okay then, see you on the terrace in an hour."

IT WAS THE last week of July, when Matt contacted Aldo to meet him at the abandoned monastery of Agio Deka, on the south side of the mountain. Aldo had arrived early and was waiting, in an irritable mood, as he hated being summoned by this once friend now turned nemesis. His dislike for Matt intensified as the minutes ticked by, when he finally spotted his car pulling-up behind him. Aldo got out to meet him half-way between their vehicles, he did not want Matt towering over him, giving him orders as he sat, low, trapped in his seat.

"Come stai, paesan?" Matt greeted him in a too warm manner.

"Cut the bull, Matt, and just give me the score. I'm not in a friendly mood."

"Okay! Okay!" Matt, still smiling, holding his hands up said, "You're all about business, and that's good, 'cause as of now, we're in business. The account in Ukraine's all set-up, and so is the first shipment from Turkey," he continued, very pleased with himself, "Crates of ersatz Beluga caviar from Romania, extra-virgin Tuscan olive oil from Tunisia,

Parmigiana Reggiano from Bulgaria, authentic Spanish saffron from the Philippines, French vsop cognac from Russia and vintage Barolo from Morocco. Oh yeah, and preserved Périgord truffles, from Oregon."

"Oregon?" Aldo said, dropping his guard for a moment.

"Yeah, seems they can grow them there, commercially, by inoculating their fir trees. Food snobs won't have them, so we give them what they want…it's just not what they think they want," he laughed.

"So, it's all counterfeit?" Aldo asked.

"No, some of it's genuine, just not genuinely ours, on account of its unfortunate fall from the back of a truck. Finders, keepers, right?"

Aldo ignored the question, "I've arranged for a small-freight vessel to pick up the goods in a secluded cove about five kilometres from the ferry dock. So, the truck rolls off the dock, makes it to the cove where the cargo will be unloaded, and shipped to a receiver in Albania, who'll pay c.o.d." he handed Matt an envelope with a map and other details.

Matt exchanged it for his own envelope containing Voula's papers and further instructions. "Albania? Since when have you had friends in Albania?"

"I don't, an acquaintance does. Has an uncle there who owns the ship, knows the contacts, is reliable, has a tight mouth. There'll be no trouble."

"You know that granddaughter of yours is a little troublesome, has quite a mouth on her too. But I like her, stands-up for herself."

"Yes, she does, and so will I if I have to. Just don't you or that smarmy nephew of yours give me any cause."

"Wow, what a hero. Quite the family guy, eh, Aldo," Matt mocked.

"What do you mean by that?" Aldo challenged, stepping forward.

"Dunno, just thinking about your dear, departed mother," Matt grinned.

"Shut-up about my family! I took care of my mother," Aldo shouted.

"You sure did!" Matt laughed.

Enraged, Aldo, punched him sharply in the mouth, but not nearly as hard as he really wanted to, fearing he'd go too far.

Matt stumbled back, surprised, hurting, his lip beginning to swell. "What the fuck! I'll get you for this,' he backed off towards his car, "Just watch your back, cause you're gonna pay!" Matt shouted, slamming the car door, peeling off towards town.

Aldo stood quiet for a moment, nursing his

knuckles, regretting his actions, worrying that maybe Matt might take it out on Jesse. He was desperate to get her away from Matt, and the crowd on that ship, but neither he, nor Voula had any idea how. The only consolation being that there were just three weeks left before she returned to Canada. Then he could relax. In the meantime, he headed home, to take care of business.

JESSE WAS JUST getting ready to leave for work when Aldo came in. Voula was putting the last pins and hair clip on Jesse's chignon.

"There now, you're ready for the ball, princess," Voula said, smiling. "Doesn't she look glamorous, Aldo?"

Jesse did a little turn for him, then put on her gold-mesh, Elsa Peretti earrings, a gift from Peter.

"Huh," he said grumpily appraising his granddaughter's appearance, "Does the back of that dress have to be so tight, and the front be so low? You can see everything god gave you! You look like a tart."

"What did you just say?" Jesse said, indignantly.

Voula jumped in quickly with, "Why would you say such a nasty thing? Apologize. NOW!"

Aldo hesitated a moment, looked down, aware

that he was out of line, but still feeling angry that Jesse was so naïve. "Okay, I'm sorry. I shouldn't have said that. It's just that I'm not used to seeing you like this, you never dressed like that before. I'm afraid you'll attract the wrong attention. You know, the wrong kind of men. I just want you to be safe."

Jesse, still angry, responded firmly, "I've been dressing 'like this' for quite awhile. And I can take care of myself. So, then I guess I can add idiot, to tart, in your assessment of my character?" She turned to Voula, "Thanks for your help, I'll be back really late, so don't wait up." She left the room as they could hear the sound of the La Medusa tender pulling up to the dock.

Aldo went to the window, watching as Peter helped her on to the boat, then sped away, as Voula remonstrated, "What on earth was that all about?"

"Like I said, she looks like a tart. I hate that she plays along with them doing that to her to gratify their jumped-up, creepy clients. I worry about her attracting the wrong kind of attention, she's not as savvy as she thinks."

"Yeah, okay, but you don't have to literally call her a tart. She doesn't see it the way you do, I think she's just having a bit of fun. Anyway, Peter's there, he's not going to let anyone get out of line with her."

"Peter? Ha! He's the one I'm most worried

about," Aldo responded, grabbing his keys, making for the door, "I'm going to work."

"What about dinner? I got some steaks."

"Save them for tomorrow, grab a cab later, come to the restaurant, we'll eat together there." He turned back to give her a peck on the cheek, "And look, I'm sorry, okay? I'm just a little stressed. See you later."

Voula sighed wearily, sat on the couch, and reached for her tarot deck, *Well I guess it's just you and me now, and you better start talking,* she whispered to herself, as she thoughtfully shuffled the cards. When they felt 'ready', that is tight in her hand, resistant to more shuffling, she spread-out her purple cloth, placed a rose quartz crystal at the top and laid out three cards side-by-side:

Hmm, the eight of wands, Magician – reversed, Emperor – reversed. Well, well, looks like there's some fast-moving energy coming in from a deceptive, maybe criminal source, and someone's being a bully, a tyrant, but who?

Let's see, give me clarification, Spirit, who, what, when, even? Voula thought, as she shuffled again and laid-out the first card below and between the eight of wands and the magician. *The three of wands, so something from across the water? From a ship perhaps? This fast energy, now looks like missiles…she* drew another card, placing it between the magician and the Emperor, *The tower! Like lightning, everything's coming down for the emperor, but when?*

The next card she laid alone on the third row, *Strength! The lion, Leo, everything's going to come down during August, the time of Leo! But who? Spirit, who?* She implored as she drew another card and laid it on top of the last one, *The chariot, that's Aldo's card and a card of war. Tell me more,* she pulled another, it was *the six of swords, hmm, more boats, water, someone's pulling away from turbulence.*

Okay Spirit, one more message please, Ah! the Ace of swords! Victory... for Aldo? Please, god, let it be for Aldo.

Voula picked-up her cards, shuffled them, passed the crystal over them to cleanse, then replaced them in the box, as she ruminated on the messages received. She now knew there was a deceptive element, an abuse of authority, fast, destructive energy breaking it down, and a strong push forward away from the chaos, into calmer waters and victory over oppression. All to go down in August...*what's happening in August to do with boats, explosions, war? Of course! The Varkarola festival, August eleventh.*

Yes, they told me about it at the salon; the miracle

of Saint Spyridon who saved the island from the Turkish invasion. There's going to be a sail-past along Palaiokastritsa bay, a mock naval battle, with cannons and everything, and Melina said, at the end they set a boat on fire, then there's a huge fireworks display.

So, it seemed there was going to be more to this re-enactment than a mock battle, someone was going to have a real war. She looked forward to the time with a mixture of anticipation and dread.

Chapter Five

I T WAS EIGHT o'clock by the time Voula arrived at the Asteri to join Aldo for dinner, and she found the place was packed. He had set aside a small table on the patio for them, their usual spot.

This was Voula's favourite space in the restaurant. At its centre stood a white, wrought iron fountain, colorful flower petals and candles floated in each of its three clam-shell tiers. In the four corners, beneath the pergola, stood faux-marble statues of the Four Graces, in the spans between them were potted palms decked with fairy lights.

The round tables were laid with white linen, topped by blue accent cloths, the large white napkins embroidered with the Asteri name, in blue. The dinnerware was classic white and the cutlery of decent quality. On each table, candles flickered in glass stem votives. Lights were woven in and around the red bougainvillea on the pergola above, the quiet strains of cool jazz set the mood.

Voula looked-up as Aldo approached with an

antipasto platter, some warm pita and a small carafe of cool retsina. "I thought we'd start with this,' he said as he laid down the food and sat with relief, "Oh, that feels good. My dogs are tired, and it's not even near closing!"

"You need new shoes, ones with good insoles, I'll go to town tomorrow and get you a better pair," Voula said, pouring him some wine.

"Thanks, you're a gem."

"I know," she said with a smile. "It's so busy to-night, you should've said, I'd have come earlier to help out."

"No need, it's all under control. Say what you like about any Europeans' service, the Greeks have them beat, they know how to treat a customer, no matter their mood. Real pros and hard workers too," Aldo said, dishing-out the antipasti.

"You're lucky that way. Especially in having Ni-kos, he treats you like family, looks after you."

"What? Looks after me? I can take care of myself; I look after him,"

"Right," Voula said with a chortle.

Just then two men arrived and were seated at the table behind Aldo. Voula caught a glimpse of them, it was the Russians she had seen in town. She watched them with what she hoped was discretion, dying to catch some of their conversation. After a minute of perusing the menus, one of them snapped his fingers for service, and Voula leapt up.

"No, Voula, Alexis will see to them," Aldo said waving for her to sit down.

"It's okay, I'm here now," she said, moving towards their table, then trying to sound American, she asked, "Ready to order?"

The taller of the two, the one she thought of as a Cossack, fired-off their requests without looking-up. When Voula returned to the table after giving the kitchen the order, she asked Aldo to trade places with her.

"What? Why?" he protested.

"Sh! Just do it," she whispered. Voula winced as Aldo scraped his chair on the patio stones, but the ambience was so abuzz with diners' conversations it was barely heard. She slipped surreptitiously into his seat, and took a long gulp of wine, trying to seem nonchalant.

"What's the matter with you tonight? You're acting weird," Aldo said, as he wiped up the olive oil on his plate with a morsel of pita.

"I'm fine, better than fine, just in a good mood. I want to sit here, because I like to see the room, who's here and watch who's coming in. I've already seen the water view and the marina," she smiled, a little too brightly.

"Uh-huh," Aldo said unconvinced, but decided to let it slide, "What do you want for a main?"

"Mm, let's see. How about the grilled sardines and an Asteri salad? And you, you must be starving, you didn't have much breakfast."

"I am, so I'll have the lamb chops with roast potatoes," he said, hailing their server.

Voula seemed distracted as they waited for their orders, and Aldo made small talk, she was straining to hear the Russian's conversation, they were speaking low, and not saying much of interest, when Voula heard the snap of fingers again, she rose to attend them.

"Yes?"

"Wine," the Cossack indicated the bottle he wanted from the list.

"Right away," Voula left for the bar, and fetched the bottle. She performed the usual ritual of pouring an ounce for tasting, it was pleasing. This time, the Cossack looked-up at her, and gave her a hard stare, as if he'd seen her somewhere. Voula poured the wine, and quickly returned to her seat.

"What was that about? Leave service to the staff tonight, alright? I only have about another half-hour before I should go back to the kitchen, so please, quit being a jack-in-the-box!"

"Sorry, it's just that I want to be helpful."

"You are, just by being here with me, okay?" Just then, their meals arrived, "Let's eat. I'm starving. And Alexis, a glass of the red burgundy and the white for Voula, thanks."

As they tucked into their meal, Voula continued to eavesdrop. At first, it seemed the Cossack was sulky, complaining to his companion about their lack of progress, he was blaming him for not being tough enough.

The other man became angry, banged his fist on the table, and raised his voice. Voula leaned back, trying to catch what the argument was about. *They're going to teach someone respect, it's their turf and they want what's owed them, she can't ignore them anymore, not after Varka–*

Just then, nearby, an overly animated guest sent a carafe crashing over the edge of the table, spraying red wine on the pant's leg of the Cossack, who leapt-up in anger.

"Opa!" the rest of the guests cheered.

Damn! Voula said under her breath. *Varkarola, I was sure he was going to say, after Varkarola. But why? And who is the 'she' they were talking about?*

A WEEK LATER, Jesse had the day off, and was going to join Voula for lunch on the terrace, after completing some calls home to Toronto. She had been a while, Voula could still hear her talking, rather loudly, so not wanting to interrupt her conversation, decided to put their lunch back in the fridge. Then filling the watering can, she topped-up the pretty concrete birdbath Aldo bought her last Christmas.

Just as she was watching the hummingbirds buzz-by on their way to the nectar in her hibiscus, Jesse emerged, looking flushed.

"Are you okay, Jess?"

"No, not really. I need a spritzer. Want one too?" Jesse asked, on her way to the kitchen.

"Sure," Voula said, going in after her, to fetch their lunch.

Once the drinks were poured, and the first sips taken, Jesse launched into a tirade, "I swear between my meddling mom and Josh, I'll be driven to more than just drink!"

"Oh. Well, I couldn't help but hear your arguing with them. What's the crime?"

"Mom's, like I said, is meddling. Always trying to help out, the wrong person, in this case my ex, to whom she thought it was a great idea to rent my flat.

My EX! Can you imagine how awkward that is?"

Voula shook her head in sympathy, as Jesse went on, "And now, said ex has just informed me that he and one of my best friends, Kate, are 'seeing' each other. He dropped this bomb by saying he just wanted to give me a 'heads-up', his words, before I return. No other prior discussion or warning from either of them during the several months and frequent Instagrams, emails and Skype calls between us, that their status had changed. They're such cowards, especially that little rat, Josh. Ha! Maybe skulking around my parents' basement is just where he belongs." Jesse drained her glass and went for a refill.

Voula, trying to smooth things over, offered, "Perhaps they've just started seeing each other romantically, and there was nothing to say earlier about it?"

"I doubt that."

"Then, look at it this way, Jess. If they'd told you earlier, it would've cast a shadow over your time here, thinking about them, how close they might be getting. I know, it's hard to let go of an ex. But you should just let him go," Voula advised as she picked-up a forkful of peperonata.

"You're being too reasonable, Voula. All I want right now is to be very mad!" Jesse retorted, scrunching-up her paper napkin and tossing it onto the table, in disgust. She took a pause, then said quietly, "One of them…no, both of them should've told me they were dating, just out of respect." Then leaning back in her chair, closing her eyes to the heavens, "Why does this keep happening to me?"

"What specifically?"

"The best friend with ex-boyfriend thing, and I'm afraid it's becoming 'a thing'. Be my BFF, and don't worry if you're single, 'cause my guy will soon be my ex and *your* next boyfriend! Shit, it's Athina and Ainsworth all over again," she grumbled, stabbing at some grilled eggplant and feta. "Why don't I ever get the happily ever after?"

"Because you don't want it, you're not ready for it. You are still in the midst of your Saturn, Uranus, Jupiter return," Voula said with conviction.

"What's that?"

"Astrologically speaking, between the ages of twenty-one to twenty-four, one experiences partial Saturn, Uranus and full Jupiter returns.

"Saturn helps you own responsibility for your choices and actions, no matter the outcome, and if you are true to yourself in making those choices, which Uranus urges, then you will embrace the future with Jupiterian self-confidence in your ability to build the life you want for yourself."

"So, then it's clear sailing from there?"

"Mostly, if you do it right, yes, until your next stage, twenty-eight to thirty, when you're hit with your full Saturn return."

"How many returns are there?"

"Seven," Voula said, re-filling her glass.

"Well, it seems like it's cycles of returns back to the future."

"I think that's aptly put, Jess."

"Thanks, Voula. I guess I really shouldn't be upset about my friends getting together, 'specially since I am seeing someone."

"How are you and Peter getting along? Any plans for after you leave, will you stay connected?" Voula asked.

"No, we haven't talked about that at all. I think we both understand the relationship is of this place and time, not a life plan. I mean, I don't even think Peter ever plans beyond next week. Haven't really asked him though," Jesse said, finishing her lunch.

"I see, you just want to keep it light, no commitments."

"Right," Jesse affirmed, checking her phone, "but, speaking of commitments, I invited Peter to the Banfield's 'afternoon cocktail do'. They're unveiling the family portrait, can't wait to see it framed and hung," she spoke while texting. "I'd better get going though, I need to get some wine in town, and Peter wants me to pick him up early."

"You go ahead, I'll clear the table. And remember to take a picture of the painting for us, we'd love to see how it looks hung too."

As Peter drove them down a narrow, winding road on the Vespa, Jesse sat behind him, cursing under her breath. She hated him being so secretive about this errand he claimed he had to do, especially as it took them miles out of their way, through clouds of dust whipped-up from the dry road, which fell in a fine mist on their clothes, making her cough and worry they'd show-up at the cocktail party looking like vagabonds. Finally, he turned off and parked in a small clearing.

"Well, what now?" Jesse asked, shaking the dust from her long silk, peasant skirt.

"Just stay here, and stay quiet, until I come back. I won't be long," he said, taking the small black valise from the back of the bike.

"What? And you're just leaving me here? Where are you going?"

"I have to meet someone on the other side of that copse, see?" he said pointing to a distant clump of shrubs and several poplars.

Jesse squinted and could just make out a glint of chrome, another motorbike parked in the brush. "I don't like this one bit, Peter!' Jesse hissed angrily.

"It's okay! The sooner I go, the sooner I'll be back. Now just go wait by the bike, and please be quiet," he said, turning to go.

Jesse did as he asked, and waited, leaning against the Vespa, arms folded indignantly across her chest, her phone tightly gripped, watching the time. They had to be at the Banfield's by four-thirty. After ten minutes passed, Jesse put her phone away, and decided to edge up to the meeting place, to see if she could catch a glimpse of Peter and his contact, and more importantly, if she might be able to hear what this was all about. When she was near the copse, she could neither hear, nor see anyone. *Hmm, he said, on the other side of here, but how far?*

Just as she made to advance further, a hand reached-out across her mouth and an arm encircled her waist. At first, she thought it was Peter, playing a joke on her, but soon realized her captor was a much bigger, stronger man. His hairy forearm, pressing against her diaphragm, was emblazoned with a familiar tattoo. He said nothing, as with one swift motion, he released her waist, pulling one of her arms up her back, frog-marching her to beyond the copse, where she saw Peter with a tall, dark, pony-tailed man. Immediately, upon seeing her, he grabbed Peter, and pulled his gun on him.

"Look what I find sneaking around," her assailant said in a thick Italian accent, as he shoved her forward.

The ponytailed man, also Italian, waved his gun at Peter, "What's this? You think we're having a party, bring all your friends, eh?"

Peter looked petrified, he swallowed hard, then said, "No, no. I told her to wait by the bike. She's just a friend, we're going out after, so –

"You thought it's good for a date?" he grabbed the back of Peter's neck and shook him. Pointing his gun at Jesse, the man asked, "Who the hell are you?"

"Nobody, just Peter's friend. He did tell me stay away. But he was taking so long, and I just had to – Jesse looked down, her lips pressed tightly together, trying to think of the right thing to say.

"Just had to disobey, stick your nose where it don't belong?" the man holding her arm yelled in her ear.

"No! No! I just…I just… had to pee!" she felt faint, and closed her eyes, not wanting to see the bullet she felt sure was coming.

The air around them hung thick and still, no one breathed, when the armed man suddenly lowered his gun, threw back his head, releasing a loud, belly-laugh. He grew weak and limp with laughter at the innocent absurdity of Jesse's response.

The man quickly recovered his composure and was back to business. Sizing both of them up, nodding to his accomplice to release Jesse, he threw a small bag at Peter, waved his gun at them both, chortling derisively, exhorting them to "Vai! Vai, ragazzi, stupido!" essentially, 'get lost kids', in Italian.

They got the point, and dutifully, quickly, headed-off to the bike, without looking back. Peter got on first, Jesse, close to tears, jumped on behind, and held-on tightly. Peter's shirt was damp, he was shaking. He gunned the engine and sped recklessly out of the clearing onto the empty road. After several kilometres, and being sure no one was following, Peter pulled over in a layby to see how Jesse was.

"Don't come near me, Peter!" she shouted, her face livid, her make-up smudged from tears. "You're in the Camorra...*aren't you*?"

He said nothing, looked imploringly at her, standing a few feet away, his arms, hanging limp at his sides.

She advanced, menacingly, her arm rigid, pointing at him, "You are! Admit it! You're a low-life gangster...a fucking drug-dealer!" she continued to shout.

"What? No, no," he replied in a soft voice, shaking his head, stepping towards her, "You watch too much tv, little girl."

"I am not a 'little girl'! I saw the tattoo on that prick's arm and on your shoulder, why would anyone who isn't in the Camorra carry the mark of a member?

"How do you know it's a Camorra symbol?"

"I Googled it," Jesse countered, suddenly feeling foolish.

"Oh, and what did the great god Google tell you?" he asked, seeming amused.

"That the 'Sacra Cortona Unita' the bleeding heart and crown of thorns on your tattoo is a symbol of the Camorra in Naples."

"Excuse me, but I'm not Neapolitan," Peter smirked, flattening his hand against his heart.

"Oh, get real! The Camorra is international, just like the Mafia and the 'Ndrangheta," Jesse replied with disdain.

"Wow! You really have been doing your homework," Peter remarked, thumbs in his belt loops, leaning back on his heels.

Jesse was face to face with him now, "Stop talking down to me Peter! God, you are such an asshole! I know what's in that bag. I have eyes and ears; I can see and hear what's going on on that boat too."

"Oh, and what lovely eyes and ears," he said mocking, when she side-stepped in, slugging him hard, putting her shoulder into it, like Aldo taught her, a left up-jab to the side of his jaw, he didn't see it coming…

Peter reeled back, "You little bitch!"

Jesse stood her ground, her jaw clenched, clasping her throbbing fist, determined not to cry out. She just stood there, stone cold silent, waiting for his next move.

He rubbed his jaw, "Christ, my face hurts." Then rubbing his temples, "Now my head is pounding."

Satisfied that he wasn't going to retaliate, Jesse apologized, "I'm sorry, I just lost it. This is serious, and you're treating me like an idiot. If it's any consolation, my hand is killing me," she said, trying to shake off the pain, her livid knuckles beginning to swell.

They both laughed a little. Then stayed silent for several moments, when Peter said, "Look, you did your job, got good money, great tips, no one was mean, no one was inappropriate, so what's your beef, really?"

"Money laundering…drug running …famous paintings…stolen. A politician's boat blown-up, who was anti-Camorra. It's no secret, it's all in the news. And those creepy Russians, from the other ship that keeps dogging us, when they tried to board, security was all over them, that was pretty intense. And now you're using me to pick-up drugs?"

Jesse looked at Peter sternly, pausing for a moment… "And that girl, the one you told me you fired for being drunk and light-fingered, she was the one in the posters in town, wasn't she? She wasn't fired, she disappeared. Did la Medusa disappear her?"

"What? Whoa now! That's quite an imagination you have! She disappeared because she wanted to, some people just want to disappear, alright? 'Poor little rich girl', hated her family…

"Look, I never should've hired her, the background check showed trouble with stolen credit cards, but she gave me a sob, saying it was because of abuse from her parents, and she'd been clean for ages.

"So, I trusted her story, convinced Matt to give her a chance and that was how she repaid me, by running off with money and anything else she could grab from the ship and crew. Happy now? Or do you prefer your fairy tale where Peter is the big, bad, wolf?"

Jesse, unconvinced, carried on, "You dragged me into this, nearly got both of us killed. I don't want any part of this anymore."

"Oh, so now you're a Mafiosa, a moll, part of 'la

cosa nostra'? Don't be absurd, you're not part of anything."

"Not now, but you and the rest of them are. I see those guys flying-in on the helicopter with their big black briefcases. Full of money and drugs, aren't they? Don't give me any more bullshit!" she backed away towards the bike, "And those paintings la Medusa says are reproductions, that's a lie too, isn't it?"

Okay, okay…look Jess, please come here," he opened his arms.

She ignored the gesture, just stood still, and listened.

"All of us, Charley, Suze, Wu-Tang …we're not organized crime members. We're just people, like you, who want to earn good cash, to get a stash for 'the someday'. For Suze and Charley, someday's a raw bar in St. Thomas. For Wu-Tang, it's home to Samoa, buy land, and become a developer."

"And you…" Jesse looked at him sideways, caring just enough to be curious.

"For me, someday, soon, getting a boat to hunt treasure, in Costa Rica. I know just where too, Jess. I've been studying marine archaeology for years while doing this gig, and I think I know where the next big find will be," he said, his eyes brightening, his voice full of enthusiasm.

"So, Captain Hook, … a treasure hunter, eh? What about your membership in clan Camorra?"

"What membership? My tattoo and all that initiation voodoo, that's Uncle Matt acting out his Robert DeNiro fantasy. Wants to be a big man, when all he does is tote and fetch for la Medusa. He made me do this Camorra shit to get the job.

"I hate that old wop world, the old farts' secret club! I don't have anything to do with it, I've never hurt anyone, never carried a gun, I keep my head down, and get on with my job. Until I have enough money to get on with my real life."

"As a fortune hunter?" she said derisively.

"Yes…you'd love it, Jess. We could have a great life together," Peter pleaded.

Jesse winced; he suddenly seemed embarrassingly naïve. She walked calmly to the bike, dampened a tissue, and wiped-off her streaked mascara.

"So? Are we going to the party?" Peter asked, making to join her.

"I am. Not sure where *you're* going though," she said, mounting the bike, "Up to you, I guess, but this is your last stop on my journey," she said revving the engine.

"What are you doing? You can't leave me here! C'mon Jess, don't be an idiot–

She didn't hear what else he shouted as she sped

away, leaving him in a cloud of dust.

"Goodness gracious, girl! You look like you've been dragged backward through a hedge."

"Oh shush, Harry. What a way to greet our guest of honor," Claudia said, as Janita showed her in. The other guests had arrived and were already chatting and drinking, as Jesse apologized for being late.

"Never mind that dear," Claudia said taking her arm, "what's this? Your poor hand and arm are all bruised, we need to get some ice on those. Come with me," she led the way to the kitchen.

Jesse, reluctant, said, "I don't want to take you from your guests."

"Nonsense," Claudia retorted, getting out two cold packs from the freezer. "When you have rambunctious grandchildren, you're always prepared." She pressed the packs on Jesse's arm and hand. "Now, tell me what happened. And where's your friend?"

"He couldn't make it. So, I went to get some wine at the Bodega in town, you know they have a steep step down into the store?"

"Oh yes, very precarious. You stumbled on it?"

"Missed it entirely, coming into the dark from

the bright sunlight, didn't see it at all. Cannonballed forward, tripped over the front of my skirt, crashed into the counter, tried to break my fall with my arm and hand," Jesse lied convincingly.

"At least the only thing you broke was your fall! Now, you just stay like this for a bit, while the swelling goes down, the powder room off the kitchen has bandages and Tylenol in the medicine chest, if you need them. You can tidy-up there and join us when you're ready, okay?" Claudia said smiling.

"Okay, thanks. Sorry to be a bother."

"Not at all. In the meantime, I'll send-in a stiff 'G and T', for you," Claudia said, leaving to join her guests.

When her injuries looked and felt better, Jesse went to freshen-up. She pulled back her hair, splashing cold water on her face. Drying-off, looking into the mirror, she saw she had lost one of her gold Peretti earrings. Peter had given them to her shortly after they met, said they were to make up for the bruised arm he gave her at Easter. She was flattered, they were quite expensive, but now Jesse wondered if they were genuine, or like Peter, just good fakes.

She took off the orphan earring, wrapped it in a tissue, and tossed it in the bin. Touching-up her make-up, tidying her hair, she pondered the distressing revelations of the entire day, then realized what she needed to do next.

"Ah! Here's our artiste," the admiral stepped forward to give Jesse a kiss on the cheek, take her arm and lead her towards the group of guests admiring the Banford's family portrait. Everyone made flattering remarks about Jesse's work, a few couples inquired about possible commissions, but she demurred.

"Thanks for your interest," Jesse replied, "But I leave to go home to Canada in two days."

"Oh, how disappointing," Claudia said, "you'll miss the Varkarola and our evening cruise. We have champagne and a seafood buffet as we sail out to see the fireworks and battle. It's really a splendid show. I thought you were staying until the end of August; do you really have to get back so soon?"

"Afraid so, I need to return back to my future," Jesse said, smiling, regarding her painting, suddenly feeling very proud of the work she'd accomplished.

Chapter Six

THE SLOW BOAT TO ALBANIA

I T APPEARED AS if the heavens and the sea were in mutual reception as Poseidon, played by the tallest man in town, a six-foot-six clerk from the American Express office, waded into the shallows of Paliokastritsa Bay.

He shook his raised trident ominously, as the full moon rose above the smoke and clouds, spilling its silver beams across the water, anointing the god of the sea, as he declared the battle enjoined between the Corfiot fleet, manned mainly by local fishermen, and the invading Turks, also, Corfiot fishermen.

Smoke from flarcs, poured in plumes from the bows of the vessels in imitation of cannon fire, as noisy fireworks were enthusiastically launched to aid in the excitement, which would ultimately result in one, empty old boat being set afire. Thus, the Turks were defeated by the miraculous intervention of St. Spyridon, neatly syncretising pagan, and Christian forces.

Most of the island was crowded along the north-west coast to watch the battle. Parades, folkloric performers, and other entertainments were held on the piazzas and wharfs transformed into floating stages, where interpretive dance groups enacted the tale of the battle, local bands and DJs played and youth partied. The restaurants were doing a booming business, leaving the dining rooms at The Asteri, on the east side of Corfu, more than half-empty.

"Oh well, least you not paying full staff tonight, boss," Nikos reasoned as he leaned on the bar of the unusually quiet Lola Lounge, white bar-cloth draped casually over his shoulder.

"No, but maybe it'll pick-up around ten, in the bar anyway. Speaking of pick-ups, 'Uncle Albania' doing one tonight?" Aldo asked, referring to Nikos' wife's Albanian connection.

"Oh yes, later on. Perfect night too, quiet on our side of island, full moon, no waves."

"Good! So, payment's prompt, everything else going smoothly then?"

"Yes, boss, everything is smooth," Nikos smiled.

"I don't really mind it's slow tonight, so the young ones can have fun. They've worked hard all season, deserve a little break," Aldo said, pouring Nikos a shot of ouzo.

ALDO'S YOUNG STAFF weren't the only ones enjoying a break, most of the crew of the La Medusa was on shore leave, as her mistress was away while the ship was being cleaned and polished from stem to stern. The skeleton staff that night was the captain and his relief engineer, three security guards, one cook, two housekeepers, a janitor and management, which was Matt and a sulky, off-duty Peter.

"Why don't you lay-off that crap? They don't call it dope for nothing you know, it'll rot your brain cells, and trust me, you haven't many to spare! Anyway, what'd I tell you about using on board?"

Peter ignored his uncle's rant as he sniffed-up more cocaine from the side of his fist.

"Take the zodiac out and meet up with Wu-Tang, have some real fun, gloomy guts," Matt said, pushing Peter's legs off his desk, shooing him to the corner club chair.

"I don't want to risk meeting Jesse, she's probably out at the disco wharf, where Wu-Tang'll likely be too."

"So what? You can patch things up before she leaves. Hey! Maybe even hook-up too," he said grinning.

"That's highly unlikely, as she seems to have blocked me in every way," Peter said, frowning, folding his arms, neither of them aware that Jesse had already returned to Canada.

"You only have yourself to blame. You've well and truly screwed that all up. It took me a lot of smooth talk to get the Gorgon to change her mind about having you 'walk the plank'.And you managed to do our private enterprise no favors either, I just hope Aldo doesn't decide to step out of line, blackmail will only go so far with him, I think."

"I don't care about either of them, the Gorgon, or Aldo. I want out, Matt. I'm leaving at the end of the month, going to Costa Rica."

"What? You can't just walk away, there's consequences, for both of us. Don't think I'm going to let you drop me in it, leave me holding the bag for you. You're in too deep and know too much. So just scuttle that fantasy. You're stuck with me, boy," Matt barked, sitting upright.

Then, taking-in a deep breath, softening, he said, "What you need is a break, a get-away. Find some nice, easy company, hire a little yacht, and go for a sail to some of the other islands. I can fix it up for you. You've been too long on this scow, you need to forget about that girl and get on top of another one, fast. Plenty of talent around, just stay away from the locals."

Before Peter could protest, the ship's siren went off.

"What the hell is that? Captain didn't say anything about a drill tonight," Matt said, annoyed, calling the bridge. "We're what? Okay, is security up there? I'll send Peter too." Matt hung up.

"Send me where?" Peter asked, getting to his feet.

"To the main deck, it sounds stupid, but the bridge thinks we're under attack. I'm sure it's just a few stray fireworks. Go check it out, see what security's doing."

Stepping out from the elevator on to the main deck, Peter was startled by a blaze of light, streaking a few metres in front of him, going over the stern, landing in the water. "What the …" he looked-up towards the helipad where two security guys were trying to put out a small fire. "Matt! We really are under attack,' he yelled into his Bluetooth, crouching down, making his way along the stern.

"By who?"

Peter stood-up and looked directly onto the deck of their assailant, where three men were loading and firing-off two rocket launchers. "Son of a bitch!" It's the Russians!"

"I thought we saw those pricks off three days ago, where in hell did they come from? The watch checked-in a half-hour ago, there was nothing in sight," Matt exclaimed.

"Whoa!" Peter jumped back as a rocket hit the railing and another hit the bridge, falling short of crashing into the control room.

The captain announced on the intercom that no one use the elevator, security, and management to begin evacuation procedure. Peter headed to the garages as two more rockets landed on the poop deck. Security was checking all the cabins, making sure no one was left behind. He tried to call Matt again, assuming he was still in the office, but got no answer, so told security everyone was accounted for who was staying with the ship, and that they should go now.

Peter saw them and the crew onto the two tenders, leaving the submarine for himself, and the zodiac for the engineer and captain who were staying with the ship, trying to get her out of the firing range, and into port as soon as possible. But maneuvering around the chaotic mock battle was proving difficult.

When the last of the crew and security were launched safely away, Peter went to the office in search of Matt, who he found kneeling in front of the safe, stuffing papers and stacks of cash into a large carry-all, his coveted Beretta 93R semi-automatic lay on the desk.

"Why weren't you picking-up? Hey! What're you doing down there?" Peter said anxiously, leaning over the desk at his uncle.

"Cleaning out the safe, idiot. Now's our chance, you wanna get out of this operation? Well, so do I. This ship is going down before it ever reaches port," he said, handing him the bag. "So, we're getting into that submarine and disappear.

"Take this, and put the gun in there too, then ditch your Bluetooth and your cell phone. Now! Move it!" he barked at a stunned Peter, as he made to follow his uncle's orders. Then, picking-up the gun, feeling its weight, Peter hesitated, he had certainly handled and fired guns before, but never one of this quality and caliber. "Is this thing loaded?"

"What do you think, genius?" came Matt's snarky reply, as he groaned, and stiffly maneuvered onto the chair. "Where's security?"

"Evacuated…just us on board, the engineer and captain," Peter responded, distant, running his hand along the frame and barrel of the gun. He slowly backed away, to stand against the opposite wall.

Swivelling to check the monitor showing the action on deck, panning the camera to starboard, Matt exclaimed, "Well I'll be," as he watched the Russian behemoth fire off another rocket into the bow before disappearing beneath the water. "It's a submersible! The sneaky bastards, that's why nothing was detected on watch. Looks like they're headed west," Matt said, looking-up at Peter, who firmly gripped the Beretta with both hands, aiming at his uncle. He fired a shot to Matt's chest, then another to his head. Then, Peter stood for a moment, back still braced against the wall, feet still planted apart, gun still aimed at his now dead target.

Narrowing his eyes, staring intently at the crumpled figure, his blood and gore splattered on the wall behind him, all over the monitor and desk. He wondered why he fired twice. *Does anyone ever just shoot once? Huh, maybe pros, they'd only shoot once.*

Deafened by the ringing in his ears, the acrid stench of gunpowder filling his nostrils, Peter's head began to pound. Putting the still warm gun into his pocket, rotating his neck and shoulders, releasing the tension between them, he felt himself smile a little.

Leaving the office, locking the door behind him, Peter headed for the garages. Then, turning back, remembering his uncle's command, ditched his Bluetooth and cell phone overboard.

As the submarine's hatch closed above him, Peter grabbed the console, and began to engineer his descent. "You sure you know what you're doing?" he could almost hear Matt asking warily, the first time he took him down with him. Exhilarated by the adventure of escape, he began laughing, and said aloud, "Kind'a late to underestimate me now, Uncle Matt!" Hitting the playlist he used to listen to during training; the theme from 'Jaws' flooded the bubble.

Peter cut the headlights, not wanting the Russians to see him heading east, around to the other side of the island, to Gouvia, and Aldo's wharf, across the bay from The Asteri.

"And since this tub only goes three knots an hour," Peter mumbled to himself, switching from GPS to the inertial navigation system, "it'll take about three hours, if the tide's with me."

He checked the battery was fully charged, good for up to twelve hours of power and oxygen, and even if something unforeseen happened, the sub wouldn't sink, but automatically float to the surface. When the monitor showed he was clear of nearby vessels, Peter turned-on the lights and cruised two-thousand feet beneath the water's surface.

Sitting comfortably in the air conditioned, acrylic bubble, nestled between two jet-propulsion pontoons, he felt a sense of unreality, shutting-out all thoughts of what he'd done to his uncle, and the surreal mess the contents of his exploded head and chest made all over the wall, desk and floor. Leaning back, closing his eyes, all the pressures and anxiety seemed to magically lift from his life, as if his dark, fairy godmother had answered his prayers.

Aldo can get me off the island undetected. No one connects me to him, thank god, cause the Gorgon'll have the hounds out when she sees how much I've taken. Which by the looks of it, I reckon to be about a million, give or take a few thousand.

Peter began to feel anxious, "A million? Yeah…she'd be really mad at that." He went quiet, trying to concentrate on navigation while imagining his future, on the run. His heart raced, his palms started to sweat, suddenly he felt claustrophobic.

"Relax, kid. you'll be okay. You're not alone, you can persuade Jess to come with you," he talked aloud to himself, patting the case beside him. "We can get new passports, so we can settle wherever. For all the rest of the world, Jesse Ponti and Peter Olivera will no longer exist. Now, lets get some nice cruising music." Settling on David Bowie, he took out his last packet of cocaine.

AFTER NEARLY THREE hours, the submarine entered Gouvia Bay. To minimize the risk of detection, Peter thought it best to cruise submerged, to as close as he judged Aldo's dock to be, before attempting ascent. Finally, close by, he could see lights on at the house and the dock. He pulled in and climbed out of the hatch, relieved to be able to stretch and breathe-in the fresh night air.

What to do with this now? Peter thought.

After a moment's consideration, he went back down to get the control console. Emerging, leaving the hatch open, Peter pulled the joystick…*Just like a Gameboy, easy.*

He watched, satisfied as the sub gurgled slowly down beneath the water, throwing the console in after it.

Peter looked back up to the house, hoping Jesse was in. Assuming Aldo was probably still at the Asteri. *Bet that Voula's there, though. Well, there's only one way to find out,"* he thought heading up towards the house.

Voula stood on the terrace watching the figure approach, *what was he fiddling with on the dock and where's his boat?* Then she heard them knock and decided at least to go to the door, if not open it. *I wish we had a guard dog, a nice big Rottweiler. I keep telling Aldo we need more security.* "Yes? Who is it?" she asked through the door.

"Peter."

"Jesse's not here, she's gone home to Canada," Voula replied, reluctant still to open the door, as she didn't like this Peter character at all.

"Is Aldo here? I need to see him."

"No, he's at work. You can go see him there."

Becoming impatient with this exchange, Peter pressed her, sounding urgent, "No, I have no transport. Just let me in, please, so I can wait."

Voula, against her better judgement, opened the door.

"Thanks, so much Voula. I'm really stranded," Peter pleaded, pushing past her.

Voula led Peter to the terrace and offered him a beer. He stood, sweating, rocking from foot to foot, as he explained about the explosion, the submarine escape, lying that the propellers malfunctioned, and he just made it to her dock, before the battery ran out and it sank. He noticed Voula's suspicious gaze on his bag, "And just lucky, I saved all the important documents. Didn't get time to scan them into the system, you know how governments love their paperwork, eh?"

"Is that right?" Voula responded, arching an eyebrow.

"Sit down, and have your beer, here, I'll join you, although I'm sure you'd much rather have a shot of whiskey," Voula laughed, relaxed, eyeing the anxious young man before her.

"Yep, it's been quite a night," Peter took a swig from his bottle, "so, when did Jess leave?"

"Two weeks ago, unexpected, but for the best I think."

"Yeah, I know, I'm a bad influence," Peter mocked.

"You can't say her timing wasn't good. But it's not that, I don't think Jess is so easily swayed. It's that it was time, she really felt it, the urge to move forward in her life, She'd had enough with this stop-over, didn't need it anymore."

"Right, so she set her compass and sailed off into the sunset, without me. Pity, I was hoping we could make a go of it." Peter reached into his back pocket, and pulled a gold earring from his wallet, "Here, would you please send this to her? She lost it last time we were together.

"Thought I might see her in town or around before she left, so I could return it. She looked beautiful in them, really suited her. I bought them for her hoping she'd be impressed that I had good taste."

"Sure, I'll see she gets it. I do think Jess cared for you, it's just that your lifestyle wasn't hers. But she did say how much fun you were, and that she could tell you anything," Voula said kindly.

"Yeah, she was a big talker, mostly about herself, wanting to be a world-class painter, she'll do it too. Maybe, I should've talked more about me, let her in more, would've understood me better." He leaned forward, elbows on his knees.

"I think she understood you well enough." Voula got up to peer over the railing. "Look, I think I see Aldo's boat. I'll just go down to let him in, forgot his key this morning." Voula said, wanting to get downstairs and warn Aldo about their company.

Just as she reached the door, Aldo entered, "Hi sweetheart. Glad you're still up. Good news, the La Medusa –

"Ssh!" Voula motioned upwards to the terrace, "we've got visitors…Peter,"

"Ah shit!" Aldo said, bounding up the stairs, Voula followed.

"Hey! Aldo," Peter greeted him with a hug. Then grasping his forearm, "We need to talk, outside."

"Okay," Aldo said suspecting what was coming.

ALDO LED PETER to the side of the house, then quickly turned on him, taking control of the exchange, demanded, "Where's your uncle?"

"On the boat, with the captain and engineer, La Medusa told him to stay, and send me off with this stuff from the safe," Peter said, putting his bag down on the sawhorse beside him.

"So, how'd you get here, and why here?"

"Well, I was in the sub, had trouble with the propellors, and you were close by so…"

"Oh, forget it, I couldn't get the right time of day out of you, you're so high," Aldo said, regarding Peter's glazed eyes, and dilated pupils. "Cut to the chase, what do you want?"

"I need you to get me out of here, off this island, Albania would be a start."

"Why would I do that?"

"Cause I've done you a favor."

"I thought as much, snuffed your own uncle…you little psycho."

Peter grabbed Aldo's arm, "You hated him as much as I did, so don't go asking me where to send flowers, okay." Peter released his grip, stepping back.

Aldo resisted the urge to slug him, thinking strategically instead, "I'll need all the account details for the Ukraine company and bank accounts first."

"How do I know you won't stiff me once you get them? I need insurance. Maybe I'll take Voula," Peter said stepping closer to Aldo.

"Maybe you won't!" Aldo yelled back, reaching

out to grab Peter, as he pulled a gun out of his jacket.

"Maybe I will."

Aldo felt the gun's nozzle in his belly, raised his hands and backed-off. "What are you doing, you idiot?" he rasped in disbelief. "You haven't got enough people after you? Word is the Hellenic Special Police, for many reasons, are looking for everyone connected to the La Medusa, not the least because they found a murdered body on board.

"Then there's la Medusa and friends, who'll want their money back and to shut you up. So, you're eager to get Interpol involved as well for murder and kidnapping? What's wrong with you? Didn't you get enough attention as a child?" Aldo scoffed at the desperate figure before him. Peter, speechless, put the gun down.

Then, lowering his voice, Aldo said calmly, "Look, Peter, you're paranoid, I get that, but I'm going to make a call to get you safely out of here tonight. You'll be in good hands, I guarantee it. After all, one good turn deserves another, right?" he said, smiling broadly.

"Alright, make the call, then I'll give you the Ukraine file," Peter said, returning the gun to his pocket.

Aldo turned his back, wandering a little away from him. "Yes, Nikos. Tonight, tell Uncle we have special live cargo. Yep, yep, aha. No. No, just a tourist, passing through. He'll need communication and accommodation for the night. Yes, payment, no problem. I'll bring him, you meet us there too…I don't know, Nikos, just tell her you forgot to lock a door or something, and you need to go back. Alright, good, see you then." Aldo hung-up, "It's all fixed."

Peter came forward, "I want to know names, and places."

"No names, just Uncle Albania, that's all I know, and they don't always drop in the same place, when you get there, they'll take you to a safe house and you'll have a burner phone. Meantime, get your bag, the Ukraine file, and wait in the car."

Aldo told Voula he was taking Peter to a boat to get away to another island. He'd be back shortly. Then, he called Nikos again, "Listen, forget earlier, just tell Uncle he's carrying heavy luggage, he should help him with it. Yes, very special treatment for him. This young guy, he likes exercise, so just keep him running. See you shortly."

AFTER NIKOS AND Aldo saw the unwelcome visitor off to Albania in Uncle's rusty cargo boat, Aldo, secreting the Ukraine file away his car, turned to

Nikos, "Well, do you think your friends will take care of him?"

"Oh yes, boss, like you say, very special care."

"Good, 'cause I think his health insurance just ran out. By the way, tell Uncle Albania that we're closing out business."

Chapter Seven

AUTUMN

TIME OUT IN TUSCANY

THE CROWD, THEIR decorated paper lanterns bobbing on long sticks, accompanied by marching bands in medieval Florentine dress, their alarums blaring, their drums beating the pace, began a procession from Piazza Santa Felicita to Piazza Santissima Annunziata, led by the Cardinal of Florence. From a good distance beyond the pilgrim group, it looked as if the fantastic faces and symbols on the orange, brightly lit lanterns swam macabrely disembodied, in the opaque, dark sea of the Florentine night.

September seventh is the Festa della Rificolona, or the Festival of the Paper Lanterns, lit in honor of Our Lady, the Virgin Mary whose birthday is September eighth. Their light, a symbol foreshadowing the light that Mary would bring into the world, the light of God's mercy, embodied in her son, to redeem mankind, or so the Christian faithful believe.

But the young children of the town, believed it more fun to blow spitballs from their peashooters at the lanterns, trying to knock the lights out of this particular celebration, as they had, observing their own childish tradition, for centuries. Equally irreverent, is that as much as the 'rificolona' was dedicated to Mary, our virtuous Lady, the Florentine slang applies the same term to an over-dressed, over made-up one, implying something less than virtue.

"Ow!" A spitball caught Lidia on the cheek, nearly causing her to drop her lantern. "You little devils." She scanned around for the culprit, raising a hand to the spot, now a little swollen and pink, rubbing it gently.

Antonio snoozed in his stroller, oblivious to the noise and activity around him as Nick guided them to the edge of the procession and into the Piazza Santissima Annunziata, a handsome space. Three cream and grey renaissance facades fronted the piazza, their classical loggias warmly lit, their delicate columns, supporting graceful, swooping arches framing them, as elegant stages, waiting for a medieval tableau or pageant to emerge.

"Giambologna's imposing, equestrian bronze of Grand Duke Ferdinand 1 de' Medici overlooked the proceedings. The cardinal spoke about the miracle of the Virgin's birth, the sacrifice of her son, then led them all in prayer. Antonio began to fuss, and Nick moved the stroller back and forth to quieten him down.

The Ponti family had been in Florence for just one week, and Antonio, as they expected, was having difficulty in adjusting. In fact, Nick and Lidia were just getting used to life in the city themselves, it's one thing to be a tourist, quite another to have to settle in for six months with a young child. Having seen enough of the celebration, which would go on to the Piazza del Duomo, the family headed home.

Nick put Antonio down, while Lidia sat up in bed with a brandy, writing down her impressions of the evening in the hand-tooled, leather-bound journal Nick bought at the Leather School of Santa Croce established behind the church from which it derives its name.

She ran her hand over the dark blue cover, so soft and sumptuous. Closing her eyes, she felt the embossed motifs, picturing them in her mind's eye…arabesques ran around the edges, a lace web, with a large, stylized spider, upside-down in the middle. It alluded to a story about Odin, who when hanging upside-down from the tree of life, encountered a spider spinning a web spelling-out the runic alphabet. Hence, the spider became the symbol of writers, Nick explained when he presented it to her for their anniversary.

She'd never thought of keeping a journal of their 'time-out in Tuscany,' but embraced the idea. Something to show Antonio when he grows-up.

She wrote quickly, rambling on about the startling beauty of Florence, which she'd forgotten somehow. How different it felt to see it every day, and the magic of the religious lantern festival that night, reminding her, in an inexplicable way, of pagan Hallowe'en in Toronto. Orange paper lanterns just had that vibe. She made a note to get one of those little picture printers tomorrow, to put pictures in with the entries as well.

Nick sat on the edge of the bed, massaging a foot, "Oh, that's better, god, my feet are sore, not used to so much walking."

"Yes, it's the stone cobbles that get me," Lidia said, as she closed her journal, taking a last sip of brandy.

"Lights out?" Nick said snuggling up to her.

Then lying in the darkness, not yet being able to fall asleep, Lidia asked, "Nick, do you think we've done the right thing, coming here for six long months?" She listened a few moments for his response when a loud snore broke the silence. She took that as a 'yes'.

"PRONTO?" LIDIA ANSWERED the buzzer, wondering who could be on her doorstep, at ten-thirty on this late October, Saturday morning.

"Signora Ponti?" a raspy, nasal voice asked.

"Si, cosa vuoi?"

"Okay, that's my Italian chat exhausted...Lidia, let me in for God's sake, I need to piss!" the now familiar voice on the other end laughed.

"Shelton!... Nick, it's Shelton!" Lidia yelled, enthusiastically pressing the button to admit him, as if the harder she pushed the quicker he'd arrive.

"Shelton? What's he doing here?" Nick asked as he shuffled-in from the bedroom, Antonio trailing behind.

"I don't know, but please, go and put some clothes on, and little man too," she said, shooing them out of the room, as she picked-up some wayward toys, flinging them in the toy basket, stopping on her way to the front hall.

Lidia picked-up a comb from the key dish on the hall table, fluffing her hair, then grabbing her emergency lip gloss, smiled into the mirror, giving her cheeks and lips a swipe of 'perfect peach', just in time to answer the knock at her door.

"Mew!" Shelton beamed, giving his friend a bear-hug, "You look radiant! Not preggers again, are you?"

"Oh, shut-up Shelton," Lidia laughed.

"Coming through!" a hasty Clive pushed past the pair, carrying a heavy box, on his way to where he saw the kitchen was.

"Hey, let me get that, Clive," a now-dressed Nick intercepted him.

"Thanks, my arms are killing me." Clive shook-off his pins and needles.

Shelton and Lidia followed them through the open-concept space to the kitchen, where Lidia greeted Clive with a kiss on either cheek. "Shelton, you should've told me you had a parcel, there's a service elevator inside the courtyard entrance.

"No matter, Clive needed the exercise, didn't you darling?"

"Not really," he said, winded, flopping down on a chair.

"No? Well, I need the loo!"

"Right through there, Shelton," Nick pointed the way.

Looking around, Clive remarked, "Lovely place you've got here, like the exposed beams, ochre walls a trifle dark though, but the stone fireplace and brass andirons are gorgeous. That large hunting scene above the couch is a nice touch. Somehow gives the place a rustic, sort of rural feel. Yes, very comfy, homey," he pronounced, smiling at them both.

"Coffee anyone?" Nick asked, making a move towards the espresso pot.

"Not for me, thanks. And I think Shelton's just despatching the 'grande' he chugged on the way over."

"I'm good too. Perhaps a little merenda… some antipasti?" Lidia offered.

Clive checked his watch, "Why not? That'd be lovely. I am peckish, and we have an hour to kill before check-in at the hotel, then freshen-up and out for a gallery tour."

"Where are you staying?" Lidia asked, setting-out the cloth napkins, best tumblers and majolica lunch plates.

"Nearby, at the Santa Maria Novella."

"Very nice," Nick said, plating-up wedges of focaccia, roasted peppers, taleggio, and mushroom frittata.

"Yes, very nice prices too!" Shelton exclaimed, entering the room, opening the top of the box they'd brought. "Now, let's see, what shall we have with our mid-morning snack? The Barbaresco? Or no, perhaps something lighter," he mumbled to himself, pulling-up a few bottles, peering at their labels. "Ah! Perfect, the flinty little '98, Vernaccia di San Gimignano. Good, and it's just cool enough, having been in the car," Shelton smiled with satisfaction, handing it to Nick to open.

"Don't you think it's a bit early?" Clive cautioned.

"Nonsense! When in Tuscany, eleven a.m., or near enough, is 'wine o'clock', by my clock," Shelton retorted.

When everyone's glass was filled and toasts were shared, they dug-in to their merenda.

Nick asked, "So, what brings you two to Florence, besides wine and art?"

"And the chance to visit with us, of course," Lidia said.

"Lush," Shelton answered, before biting into a pepper.

"Lush? What's that?"

Clive answered, "A new enterprise of his, an online fine wine and gourmet food club he started with Javi."

"With Javi? He never said anything, last time we talked," Nick said.

"Official launch is November, in time for Christmas corporate gift-giving," Shelton said. "I pitched him the idea of 'Lush' as a side-hustle to his main wholesale enterprise to retail and restaurant outlets. It's a small endeavor, but sales is sales. He's given me a decent budget to handle promotion, newsletters, podcasts, website, all the stuff he doesn't want to bother with."

"We've been here on business for two weeks. I'm actually on vacation, and 'designated driver' all week, as Shelton, our designated drunk, has been imbibing his way through the vendemmia wine festival."

"Very funny, Clive, but not far from the truth, I'm afraid. It's really been a bit of a grind, as we started north, four days at the Tutto Food Fair in Milan, along to the Veneto for three days, then across to Tuscany and the wine harvest here. Now, we have until Monday for a little rest and a visit before heading home from Rome," Shelton added.

"So, you're working for Javi full-time then?" Lidia asked.

"Yes, but I'm also doing some freelance journalism and guest blogging too. Millennials aren't the only ones in the gig economy, it's full of down-sized, superannuated old farts like me too!"

"C'mon now Shelton, fifty-three isn't exactly an old fart," Nick said, in self-interest.

"No? Well, it was to me when I was twenty-one," Shelton laughed.

Antonio, his sippy cup of pear juice in hand,

patted Clive on the knee. "Well, aren't you a bonnie lad!" he exclaimed, pulling him up onto his lap, tearing him a piece of focaccia, "and heavy too, what are you feeding him?"

"Everything, and constantly, it seems he's always hungry," Lidia said.

"That's my boy! Healthy appetite, like his dad, aren't you Antonio?" Nick beamed at his son.

Antonio responded, "Pada! Pada!" waving his bread at Nick.

"What's he saying?" Clive asked.

"It's his 'Italgish' for papa, he often runs his English words in with Italian ones, papa and dada, equals pada," Nick explained.

"So, he's adjusting well?"

"Oh yes, except for the first week, when he scrambled around the apartment, peeking under all the furniture, barking, and calling out 'Piggo'," Lidia said.

"He barks?" Shelton asked, amused.

"Oh yes, he and Pickles used to bark at each other. One would get the other going, it drove me nuts, and you Nick Ponti," Lidia pointed her fork in his direction, "started, and encouraged it!"

"I thought it was cute," Nick shrugged, grinning.

"Uh-huh, well I'm sure that's not what signora Pinna, our landlady thought when she heard him, he seemed positively wild," Lidia retorted, "raised by wolves!"

"Well then, which one is he? Romulus or Remus?" Shelton asked, laughing.

"Since we're not in Rome, Remus," Nick decided, serving himself another wedge of frittata.

"He goes to playschool three afternoons a week now, so I can get my work done. He's met new friends there, gets along with everybody really well, don't you little man?" Lidia said, blowing him a kiss.

"And Jesse? How did her Greek sojourn go?" Shelton asked, turning to Lidia.

"Great! She returned a few weeks early, with a new life plan."

"Yes, to move out on her own, when her perfectly comfortable family home sits empty! But Lidia thinks it's okay that she pays too much rent for a crummy junior one-bedroom instead," Nick said, pouring everyone more wine.

"That's nonsense and you know it, Nick! Our home isn't empty, her ex-boyfriend lives in the basement, probably shacked-up with one of her best friends. So, comfortable isn't the way I'd describe it.

"Anyway, Shelton, to answer your question, she's got a nice, sunny little apartment close to the subway, in midtown, where she's using the bedroom as her painting studio, and the living room as a bed-sitting room. It works well, she bought one of those sofa beds. And she won't be lonely, she's taken Pickles."

"I'm glad she came home early, so we could spend some time with her. I admit, she seems happier, certainly this new school is a much better fit, and she's been painting every spare moment, moved away entirely from collage," Nick added.

Letting a squirming Antonio down to roam, Clive, relieved the contention over Jesse's housing had passed, asked, "What subject matter is she exploring?"

"Portraiture, some random, some personal, very Francis Bacon in her approach. Lately, she's been sharing her works-in-progress; I've never seen such vigor, conviction and even passion, in her work before," Nick mused.

"I think it's exciting, healthy even. It seems she has a lot to get off her chest and work through. This is an important time, don't know why, but I just feel she's on the cusp of something," Lidia said, rising to clear her guests' empty plates.

She sighed, piling the dishes on the counter, then turned back to her company, "Right...well, I'm so glad you two found the time to stop by. It's just so good to see you both!" her eyes were glistening now.

"Miss Mew, we couldn't leave Tuscany without

seeing you and dropping off our early Christmas offering. There's some interesting labels in there," Shelton looked to Nick, indicating the box of wine, "you may want to visit some of those wineries while you're here. Makes a nice day's outing."

"I'd like to, thanks so much you two… Any plans for dinner?" Nick asked.

"I thought we'd all go out together, can you recommend somewhere?" Shelton replied.

"Sure, we have a nice family-run place nearby, child-friendly, and really good food, especially the tripe. How about we meet you at the hotel, say six-thirty? It's quite close, so we can walk over."

"Grand, now let's get checked-in to our room, and freshen-up," Clive said, as Shelton gave Lidia another hug.

AFTER RETURNING FROM dinner, Lidia lit a fire and curled-up on the couch, as Nick put a very tired Antonio to bed, and retired himself. She wasn't ready to sleep, wanting to cling to the warm feeling that welled-up within her, to savor the evening's tasty food, and lively conversation.

From the coffee table drawer, she took out her journal. She lifted the wide, red satin ribbon separating the ten or so pages she'd already filled, from the next thick, blank page waiting for her thoughts. Lidia wrote:

Saturday, October 18th,

Shelton and Clive dropped-by unexpectedly on their way home from a buying trip for 'Lush', Shelton's new enterprise. I'm so glad he's found something that suits him.

It's odd how elated you can feel suddenly seeing a familiar face abroad, as if you've been lost, or marooned on a deserted island, when, unexpectedly, an old friend appears, reminding you of the life you quite happily left, which now you are suddenly home sick for...that's not to say I don't love Florence, it's just what our marriage and Nick really needed. It's renewed his interest for scholarly work; he's become absorbed in new art history projects, spending much of his time with an art restorer, Enza, who, is our neighbor and grandmother of Antonio's new friend, Pietro.

His meeting her was a godsend to us both. It got him out of the house, where for the first few weeks we were here, he just moped around, cooking, eating, and imbibing too much, and driving me crazy! I couldn't get my own work done for the blog and the freelance articles I'd promised, I never miss deadlines, and won't start now. Good way to get a bad rep, and no work.

Now that Nick's busy researching in the galleries, meeting with Enza in Siena, following the progress of her work, and attending lectures, I should look for more work. I'll pitch a few more editors, now that the pressure's easing and I'm nearly finished the last piece, maybe an airline inflight magazine? Better research that tomorrow.

But back to what I miss about home…my daughter, our friends, not much winsome over former colleagues though, they're too tied-up in their work-a-day world. They're in the past, where they belong. I used to think it was sad how some retired people desperately cling to the old work environment that no longer has any use for them. I won't be that person! Although, in a very selfish way, I'm glad Shelton got the boot with me, he's such a special friend, he brings-out the rascal in me, I would've really felt the loss of him.

Two things I'm looking forward to having here are Christmas and Halloween! Who knew

the Italians would embrace this North Ameri-
can festival as much as they do? I was quite
surprised. I'm pretty sure this is a recent phe-
nomenon; I know they always celebrated All
Saints' Day on November 1ˢᵗ then The Day of
the Dead, on November 2ⁿᵈ, which are Catho-
lic feasts that Halloween has now somehow
segued into...I blame Martha Stewart, and
why not? Everyone else does.

I also read somewhere that in ancient
times, the peasants would disguise themselves
and beg at the door of the wealthy for food,
chanting, 'Per l'anima dei morti?' (for the souls
of the dead) instead of 'dolcetto scherzetto!'
(trick or treat) and if given food, they would in
exchange, pray for the souls of the benefactor's
ancestors.

Which reminds me, I have to start rehears-
ing Antonio on this new phrase, if he's to keep
up with the other kids in class tricking and
treating. Which brings me to another issue, the
costume...I gave Nick one responsibility to this
Halloween party, and that was to get our son a
costume...I asked him to do this two weeks
ago. He finally bought one yesterday, a
skanky-looking rodent outfit he claimed was

Squirrel Nutkin, from the Beatrix Potter books, as if that gave it some gloss!

It looked more like Ratatouille after a rough night in the sewers. I won't have my child go to his nursery school party dressed as a rat! I'm going to have to do serious cosmetic surgery on it, starting with stapling some Swifters to that ratty little tail. Anyway, Antonio, if as an adult you are reading this, still scarred by the shame of your first Halloween costume, you know who to blame.

Chapter Eight

REVELATION, INSPIRATION

OVEMBER, THE WETTEST month in Florence, is chilly too, with daytime highs of fifteen degrees Celsius, tolerable, pleasant even if sunny, though clammy, and close, if not. And foggy, the Arno Valley being a perfect trough to trap humidity.

Unlike its medieval rival, Siena, buffeted by fresh breezes, perched proudly atop a hill, which afforded it constant vigil against Florentine mercenaries. Now, threat of invasion comes from hordes of tourists eager to storm the gates of this tiny jewel built *'a misura di uomo'*, to the measure of a man, being not more than one-kilometer side to side.

One of its other distinctions being the bi-annual Palio, an ancient, tribal horse-race, undertaken bare back at break-neck speed round the shell-shaped campo, by something less than sportsman-like jockeys, each wearing colors of one of the ten finalists of the seventeen contrade, or districts. They risk life and limb trying to stay on their feisty mounts, which can cross the finish line, winning, with or without their rider. He who manages to win mounted, has the privilege of parading the painted, silk banner, the 'drappelloni,' triumphantly through the town.

The noisy, gawking crowds, flag-waving, parading heroes had disappeared months ago along with the summer sun, leaving Nick Ponti the somber greeting of a quiet, cold, and grey town. Stepping off the Florence-Siena shuttle bus, he pulled his blue paisley scarf close to his neck and buttoned the front of his thick Harris tweed jacket. Pretending to check his phone, he used its reflection to adjust a black, felt beret just so, over his now poetically long, salt and pepper curls which Lidia admonished him to either have shorn or keep tucked back behind his prominent ears. Ignoring the admonition and daring even to grow a tidy moustache, his new look, was to his satisfaction, the perfect image of a continental scholar.

It was a scholarly interest which led Nick, on this late autumn Friday, to the conservation studios in the basement of the Pinacoteca Nazionale, the region's preeminent public picture gallery. Hurrying along the via San Pietro, Nick regretted sleeping past the alarm and wondered if he had enough time to grab a pastry and cappuccino as he approached a brightly lit bar, but checking his watch, decided against it. Perhaps he could tempt Enza to take a coffee break with him later, in the meantime, he prayed his usually vocal stomach would stay quiet.

Nick turned into the entrance of the Pinacoteca, an extensive gallery housed in two adjacent former ducal palaces, the Palazzo Buonsignori and the Palazzo Brigidi, and spied a flash of platinum grey bob; Enza, huddled against a wall close to the entrance, her red cardigan held tightly closed with one hand, in the other a cigarette from which she deeply drew a long plume of smoke.

"Hello there!" Nick greeted her, "Sorry I'm a bit late."

Enza peered at him over electric blue, titanium half-glasses, her heavy-lidded brown eyes greeted him warmly through long, thick lashes, assuring him that she was not annoyed.

"It's only fifteen minutes," she shrugged. "Remember, now you are on Italian time," Enza said, taking one last drag of her cigarette. "I needed a break anyway. Come. I have something interesting to show you that just came in for evaluation."

Nick followed her to the basement with growing anticipation. Through Enza, he found a whole new world of Renaissance art to explore; the hidden female artists of that exalted era who laboured unsung in their families' art bottegas, few having practices or studios in their own name. Others were talented, untrained nuns, inspired by religious devotion, creating works for their convent's private devotion, or perhaps even commissions for patrons of their orders.

This quest to discover Renaissance female artists was created and supported by the aptly named American philanthropist, Jane Fortune, who, upon doing an art tour of Florence, naively wondered, "Where are the women artists?" Affronted that the art representing half the world's population was made invisible, unexamined, and unappreciated, she resolved to dig into the archives of galleries and museums, unearthing this lost legacy and fund its restoration by female restorers, funded by her non-profit organization, Advancing Women Artists (AWA) in Florence.

But their mandate, and funding would soon end. Something that deeply concerned retired art historian and restorer, Enza Falcone. So, she decided to train more restorers, to carry-on the work, expanding their activities beyond Florence, while perpetually seeking philanthropy, government, and public support. Something she found exhausting and exasperating, especially dealing with the byzantine workings of all government levels. All this left her no time for her writing, abandoning the retirement plan.

"Ciao," Nick exchanged greetings with a young art restorer, bent over her work bench, assiduously undertaking, with a cotton swab, the meticulous cleaning of a large still life by baroque painter, Giovanna Garzoni. Nick stepped-in beside her, putting on his reading glasses for a closer look.

"Interesting, looks influenced by the Flemish school, with the flies and slight rot on the peach here, and the flagging leaves of the figs. An allegory of a barren marriage…or perhaps an admonition to a profligate son for the lack of grandchildren?" Nick chuckled.

"Perhaps," the restorer responded without looking up. "We think it may be a commission from one of the Chigi family who seems to have lacked an appropriate heir, so yes, this interpretation is likely."

"Tempera, is it?"

"Yes, tempera, the colors therefore are still very vivid, but it is delicate work to clean, being on parchment, luckily this one isn't badly cracked. If you're interested in the restoration of another of her works, there's one in Florence, in the Galleria Paletina, a still-life of a bowl of broad beans, commissioned by the Medici."

"Thank-you, I'll look for it."

"And here she is! Come look, Nick," Enza said, wheeling-in a dolly bearing a five-foot piece covered in a tarp. "Voila!" she revealed a polychrome, woodcarving of Mary Magdalene, which had definitely seen better days. It was found in one of the cellars of The Oratory of St. Catherine, here in Siena."

"Well, well…this is new for you, isn't it?" Nick said, walking around the piece, observing it carefully.

"I know, we rarely get to work on sculpture, that's why I'm so excited. And not only for that, but also because of who I think the artist is."

"Oh, and who might that be?"

"It's a nascent thesis of mine" said Enza, tentatively, "but I think I may have uncovered an artist whom I call, for now, la Maestra di Milano, a woman artist who may have had a thriving bottega of her own, first in Siena, supplying some private patrons, but more usually, convents and monasteries or maybe even was a monastic herself. Then during the devastating plague of 1450, she, like many others fled the city.

"I believe she and her followers eventually established themselves in Milan. She is intriguing, as I'm sure she and her followers influence endured into the High Renaissance, retaining a very expressionistic, Gothic sensibility, which is very specifically

Sienese."

"Uh-huh, yes, I concur. It compares favourably with Donatello's unusual, late work, The Penitent Magdalen in the Bargello, which similarly lacks emotional restraint."

"Absolutely. You see, I don't believe that every patron's taste, in the sacred or secular, exclusively favored the neoclassical approach of Michelangelo and Raphael. I think many still loved the emotional immediacy of the original Gothic, but as in Masaccio, rendered technically more realistic and in a slightly more idealized way."

"Yes, I see what you mean. The trajectory being from the Proto-Renaissance style, beginning with Cimabue, developed by his pupil, Giotto, then finally, on the cusp of the burgeoning Renaissance movement, Masaccio, and perhaps enduring past it, in the work of your, 'la Maestra di Milano'?"

"That's the thesis," Enza smiled, elated that Nick seemed to embrace it without the usual, academic dismissiveness.

"What evidence, beyond this piece, do you have of 'la Maestra's' existence?"

"I have a friend, Venera, who is an assistant curator in the Pinacoteca di Brera, she has been reviewing and cataloguing the archives from this period and area. She has found pieces which have a strong aesthetic connection to this Neogothic Expressionism, quite distinct. They range from small works on panel to larger sculptures, mainly devotional images. She and I are currently working on finding textual evidence to support our thesis, but finding time and resources is an issue."

"I understand. Have you been to Milan to see these other works?"

"No, not yet. I plan to clear some time next week, four days is all I can spare from here, one day either side of a weekend."

Nick, still eyeing the work with fascination, fingering the deeply carved folds of the stylized drapery, said, "Can you come early to dinner Saturday? I think I have a proposition for you."

"Yes, what time?"

"Make it six-thirty, so we can talk business first."

"Six-thirty then. Now, I need to take some pictures of her before I begin the assessment. You can help me set-up," Enza said, walking over to the light stands. Nick rolled the sculpture over to the blank backdrop and helped placed the lights as Enza took some readings.

"You don't have to bother with that, Nick," Enza said as she saw him getting ready to take pictures with his phone. "I'll send you mine."

"Thanks, but I just want a few shots to take with

me now, for reference."

Getting what he needed, he put his phone away, then feeling his stomach rumbling, asked, "When you're done with the pictures, want to get coffee?"

"Sorry, no time. I have a meeting with the director in an hour and a half, and I want to at least get some preliminary notes on this piece, what it might need, how long, etcetera."

"Alright, then see you Saturday, six-thirty," Nick replied making his way out.

He hurried to the little café he'd spied on his way from the bus, quickly downed a cappuccino and pastry before hustling out to the station, to catch the twelve-thirty back to Florence. Just in time, he sat, winded, in the dual carriage seats, placing his valise on the seat next to him, as the bus was half-empty. He dropped his head back on the rest, squinted his eyes against the slanting sun, and laughed quietly.

How lucky am I? Enza's discovery could be big for me; to be editor and co-author of a ground-breaking book on an undiscovered female Renaissance master! One with a Gothic, non-mainstream sensibility, an artistic rebel no less! Could just be the beginning of several monographs on women Renaissance painters and the female art restoration movement. With my connections to an academic publisher, or even later, a mainstream one, I can bring these works and their creators, their times, to the general public too! 'Publish or perish' is the academic's dilemma; well, I don't plan on perishing in the weeds of academia and obscurity any longer. If I play this right, I'll be a Professor Emeritus, no more teaching, only publishing and research! This could be my breakthrough."

THE SAN LORENZO market was bustling, as Lidia balanced her bag of bread and produce on one hip, while digging into her pocket to answer her phone. It was Nick, on his way home from Siena, he wanted her to get a rabbit and some wild mushrooms to make cacciatore and mushroom risotto for Saturday dinner, oh and they were out of saffron too. He'd get the wine later.

"Thanks a bunch, I was just over that end of the market, now I have to trudge through this crowd to all the way back!" she grumbled to him.

Good! There's no line-up at the butcher's. Lidia ordered her rabbit jointed and with the head, knowing Nick would want it for the risotto stock. The wild mushrooms were just two stalls away, she bought a pound, reasoning she could dry some later, if they didn't all get used.

Now, she had just enough time to drop her purchases at home, before picking-up Antonio at the play centre. She was relieved to get to school just in time for closing, the admin were sticklers for punctuality, rightly so, since some parents were liable to take advantage. She got Antonio and thanked the teacher's assistant for getting him dressed, something parents were usually expected to do.

"Bisc! Bisc!" Antonio demanded a biscotti, as his mother struggled to get him into his stroller.

"Yes, yes, little man. Hold your horses, mommy has a biscuit right here," Lidia pulled an apricot-almond biscotti from her bag and handed it to her hungry little boy. But he was soon distracted by Alessandro, shouting and waving "Ciao-ciao", so dropped his treat.

"Ciao-ciao Sando!" he shouted and waved back.

Lidia, observing the five-second rule, picked-up the biscuit, dusted it off, and gave it back to Antonio. She was looking around for Flavia, Pietro's mother, so they could walk back home together, but she was deep in conversation with the head teacher, so Lidia decided to make a start. She wasn't too far on her way when she heard Flavia call:

"Lidia! Lidia!" Lidia stopped to let her catch-up.

"I was just talking to the head, she's looking for volunteers to help-out with their Christmas celebrations, she wants to do a combined program of music and a nativity tableau with the creche and the grade ones and twos."

"That's ambitious! What did you say?"

"I said yes, and that I had a friend whom I'm sure would just love to help out too!" she said, laughing.

"So, you put my name down, did you?" Lidia faked annoyance.

"Of course."

"Okay, but you're going to owe me some serious babysitting, friend. Oh, by the way, Enza's coming for dinner tomorrow, why don't you and Erich come too?"

"Sure, I think we can get a sitter. We'll bring some wine and pastries."

"Perfect. Now I just have to go to Gus' for some saffron, I hope he isn't in one of his chatty moods, I need to get dinner started. Do you need anything here?"

"No, I'm good, see you Saturday."

Back home now, after settling Antonio in for some quiet time in his play corner, Lidia had a precious hour to herself before starting his dinner, so made an espresso and sat down to write in her journal.

Friday, November 10th,

No rain Yesterday, and it was warm! Antonio was finally over his cold, he missed nursery school Wednesday, now he and I just had to get out of the apartment, get some exercise and fresh air, and avoid our cleaner, so we went on a long, aimless stroll.

I can't stand being at home when the cleaning lady, or any tradesperson is there working, makes me nervous, I feel awkward and self-conscious. I just can't do anything, I feel observed, which is ludicrous, and even worse, observing…like I'm 'spying' on them, to see if they're doing a good job. Although given what Voula was up to with my dad, maybe I should've!

If I told Jess, she would laugh at me and say, "Oh dear, mom, middle-class problems, middle-class guilt?" And she'd be right, mostly, but I wouldn't satisfy her smug self, by admitting it! After all, I'm from working-class immigrant stock, shouldn't that give me a pass? Lol! Yes, I'm laughing at myself now, out loud! Anyway, who cares? I hate housework, so sue me!

But I really did get a good work-out yester-

day, have the aching calf muscles to prove it too, the stone paving here is murder on the legs and feet. I don't know how the stylish Florentines wear their Gucci pumps and slick-soled Belvedere brogues without twisting an ankle.

I like this city of stone, even though it's hard edifices and roads are man-made, it's very different from home in its energy and resonance, from the asphalt, chrome, glass, steel, and concrete that bears no resemblance in its built form to its primal, elemental source. A city of stone, hand hewn, retains the life-force of the earth in which it was formed and the spirit of the hands that raised it up and shaped it to their purpose.

But there is also the bronze and marble that really is alive; here in Florence we walk everyday among the giants of myth, and religion. The saints and martyrs look down upon our deeds and seem to penetrate our deepest thoughts. I feel it strongly every time I walk around the Orsanmichele; Donatello's St. Mark, to me is especially formidable and disapproving. Stern, with his sacred gospel, unwavering in his evangelical belief.

In contrast, the artist's baby-faced, clean-

shaven St. George looks but a boy, too young to do a man's job, but determined, nonetheless, to be a brave soldier, even though it's apparent from his knitted brow, that he worries if he can. So unlike Michelangelo's arrogant, giant David in the Piazza della Signoria, so self-assured, unconcerned, he strikes a vulnerable posture, sporting his manhood, openly, casually. He peers into the distance in annoyance, impatient for the chance to strut his stuff and vanquish the enemy.

Back to the Orsanmichele – of all the saints depicted there, Verrocchio's St. Thomas and the risen Christ is my favorite. Antonio seemed to respond to it too, when I held him up for a closer look, he pointed and babbled, then listened intently, sucking his fingers, while I talked about it. I find it compelling, perhaps it's because St. Thomas seems to be stepping from our secular world into the sacred realm of Christ, enclosed in his niche.

St. Thomas is unsure of what he thinks, even hopes may be truth, does he really believe in the miracle of resurrection? So, Christ allows him a reassuring touch into his open wound. He doesn't admonish Thomas for his lack of faith, like St. Mark, or even the terrifying Moses would, Christ simply accepts Thomas' human failing and gives him what he needs to go on believing. We all fail and need reassurance to go on, acting on what we hope is truth in our life's journey, to continue believing, even in ourselves.

But enough psychologizing, is that even a word? Antonio and I pushed-on, or rather I pushed him, to the Via de' Tornabuoni, to the grand palazzo of another legendary Italian giant of creativity, Emilio Pucci, his temple housed in the fabulous palace of his aristocratic ancestors. I could only window-shop...my pretty Florentine wallet being pretty low on the kind of cash it needs to shop there. Antonio was fascinated. And Gucci, let's not forget that legend, you'd think they'd both planned their rhyming monikers as a clever marketing ploy, but no, both original and both Florentines.

All that glam, got me in a buying mood by the time we stumbled upon 9 Rosso, on Borgo San Jacopo, near the Palazzo Pitti. It sells all kinds of vintage and contemporary jewellery, clothing, and even ancient artifacts. I could browse in there all day. Now, I have finally found a little Curiosity Shop of mine own, a little sanctuary, where my imagination can wander among its wonders, and the proprietor, Paolo, is a fountain of knowledge as arcane and eclectic as his collection.

I found a gorgeous, Art Nouveau, cloisonne butterfly pin for Jesse's Christmas gift. I know she'll love it…at least, I hope she will. She and Athina were always rummaging in the charity and vintage shops for clothes and jewellery, as the fashions were more 'sustainable' and original when combined with contemporary pieces. They often asked me to make alterations, one of the few times we connected on a feminine level.

I guess I don't know what she really likes now. Jess's quite different from that young girl. It'll be okay, I'm sure she'll appreciate it, if only for its craftmanship and jewel-like colours. Yes, I'm going to send it to her, she'll wear it, …anyway, she better, because I can't take it back.

Lidia, pressing hard on her felt-tip, did a quick, expressive sketch of the pin in the margin, before closing the book and making a start on dinner.

IT WAS SATURDAY night, Michael Bublé was crooning, the fire was crackling, and the air throughout the Ponti's apartment was rich with the aromas of braised rabbit in a savoury rosemary wine sauce. While a warm, homey stock simmered away on the cooktop, the pungent scent of freshly grated parmesan was released.

"That'll do us for tonight…thanks, Flavia," Lidia said, turning away from her risotto, as she took the cheese and grater from her friend, and refreshed her Manhattan. Flavia and her husband, Erich, a Swiss investment banker, were having their cocktails in the kitchen, keeping Lidia company, while Nick and Enza enjoyed theirs in the study, in a serious, tête-à-tête.

"Look Enza, this could be a great opportunity for you and me, to build further on the legacy of the AWA, after all isn't that what you're working for?" Nick asked, sitting close to his friend, who reached into her clutch, and drew out a slim package of cigarettes. Looking for his assent, Nick responded, "Sure, go ahead. Just let me open this window first." He rose, and pushed the sash open with some effort, then placed an ashtray from the top desk drawer in front of her.

"Thanks", she said with a little smile, as he made to light her cigarette. "Ah! That's better," she exhaled, "it always helps me think." Enza paused, quiet for a moment.

"Well?" Nick asked, impatient.

"Hmm…yes, your proposition has possibilities. But so much rests on whether or not the facts and back-story behind these works add up to what we think they might."

"Of course, but there's only one way to find out and that's doing more digging, primary and secondary research, which, happily I have lots of time for."

"Yes, and I will help, but more in connecting you with the resources you'll need, people of influence, with access to private collections and archives," she said, taking a last draw on her cigarette, before stubbing it out.

"I was hoping you'd say that. Now, I would like to, if it's not imposing too much, to accompany you to Milan."

"Yes, yes, of course you should."

"When might you go?"

"I was thinking of leaving next Thursday night, returning Monday afternoon."

"Perfect! I'll just clear it with Lidia, but I can't see any problem. Now, shall we join the rest? I'm starving."

THE EVENING PASSED amicably with Lidia and Flavia deep in conversation about the upcoming Christmas pageant, local gossip, and the growing success of Lidia's blog, which Flavia, a part-time tv production assistant, thought Lidia should take to a network, as a comedy/cooking show for streaming content, and offered to give Lidia guidance on how to craft a pitch. Lidia, excited by the prospect, was seriously considering it.

Nick, Erich and Enza exchanged views on local politics and international markets, particularly the art market and the phenomenon of what appeared to be obscene amounts of money-laundering and brazen fraud.

"Well, after the oligarch's bought up all of Knight's Bridge they could, the art market, and its greedy auction houses and collectors, was the next obvious dumping ground," Erich asserted.

"Yes, and governments don't seem to give a damn!" Nick added.

"Oh, come now, Interpol uncovers the odd scandal once in awhile, small to medium fish on their hooks, and they hold it up to mainstream media as progress, when it's only a mere token," Enza laughed.

"That, my friends, will end with the inevitable global shift to the block-chain economy, which makes transactions very traceable to source," Erich replied.

"Really? You think so? You mean Bitcoin will take-off?" Nick asked.

"Bitcoin is only one cryptocurrency of many, it's not the blockchain itself. But yes, this shift is inevitable. We, in the commercial finance sector, are anticipating it. I'm not saying you should buy just now, wait, this'll take quite a few years. Right now, it's very speculative, but lucrative for day traders who know the market," he advised.

"Would anyone like more espresso?" Lidia asked, rising, hoping their guests would pick-up the signal. It was late, and she was flagging.

"No, thanks, Lidia. We should go. C'mon, Erich, remember, it's your turn to get up with Pietro tomorrow." Flavia said, reaching for her phone.

"Yes, mistress!" He gave a little bow as Nick handed him his jacket.

Enza wrapped herself up in her long, thick, woollen shawl, "Thank-you for a lovely evening Lidia. Nick, we'll touch base Monday, okay?"

"I'll be in Siena by ten-thirty," Nick responded, as their guests stepped-out into the dark, silent street, where fat snowflakes drifted lazily in and out of the dim sprays of streetlight, to settle, glistening, on the heads and shoulders of the trio, their arms linked together, hastening toward home.

When Nick finished clearing-away the coffee tray, and Lidia turned on the dishwasher, they went to bed.

"Ah, finally! I'm beat," Lidia said snuggling up to Nick.

"Didn't you have a good time tonight?"

"Sure, just tired lately. Hope I'm not coming down with Antonio's cold."

"Nah, you'd have had it by now. Maybe you're just low on iron, I'll make some cream of spinach soup tomorrow. I had a very productive talk with Enza, in fact, she invited me to Milan with her Thursday night, returning Monday. We're going to …oh, great!" Nick stopped short as he was interrupted by his wife's little snorts and snores. "Guess we'll talk about it in the morning," he muttered, kissing her cheek, turning off the light.

LONG DISTANCE CALLING

It was Saturday, seven a.m. Toronto time as Becky squinted through bleary, early-morning eyes at her phone, while Lidia, well into her day, strolled through her apartment holding-up the phone, so Becky could see each room as they chatted. This was the first time they managed to connect, beside email and Facebook over the six-hour time difference between them.

Completing her mini tour, Lidia settled into the couch, one leg tucked beneath her, one large cushion across her lap, where she rested the arm holding her phone.

"Nice digs, Lid! Looks like you've made your-selves at home," Becky remarked, stifling a yawn. "How're the neighbors?"

"Good…really good, actually. There's a family just two doors down who've become friends, we met them through their little boy, Pietro, he goes to Antonio's nursery school. His mom, Flavia, works part-time in production for a tv network, and you'll never guess what she thinks I should do!"

"What? You sound so excited; does this have to do with Kitchen Klutz?" Becky asked, taking a sip of the morning's first cappuccino.

"Yes, it does. Flavia says it has potential for streaming content as a tongue-in-cheek, cooking show. She loves my posts, and thinks my approach is quite original."

"Right…just don't get your hopes up too high,

it's tough to get a show. And would you want to host, or an actor? Hosting could be really stressful," Becky advised, glancing in the mirror, adjusting her hair clip.

"Gee, thanks, Debby Downer. The issue of hosting isn't relevant, this would be a scripted comedy series, based-on my blog, and of course, I have my hopes-up, who pitches anything without every hope that it'll succeed?"

"Okay, okay! Sorry, just didn't want you to be disappointed, that's all. But I'm sure it's a great idea… you'll likely get a positive response, eventually."

"Huh, now you sound condescending…"

Becky sighed deeply, "Oh c'mon Lidia, I didn't mean…"

"Never mind, you never were a morning person! Anyway, I didn't call to argue. How's the cohabitation going?" she said, trying not to sound peeved.

"Great. We're very happy, but very busy. Lately, I've had to be more hands-on at the company than I wanted, now that Ramona's bringing-in more business, Paul and the girls are swamped. So, I've been helping them with recruitment, which is time from the travel business, I can't really afford. Thankfully, it's down to selecting from the short-list now, then they can get some relief, but first there'll be training."

Becky lowered her voice, "Actually, I'm worried about Paul, his blood-pressure is up, he's on nsaids. And the doctor wants to put him on a waiting list for a knee replacement, which, typically, he's resisting, but there's only so much anti-inflammatory he should take, so it's got to be done."

"Oh dear, looks like you're victims of your own success. Don't worry, everything'll be better, once you get your Christmas break," Lidia said.

"I guess, I don't know what Paul and Ramona's plans are, but Javi and I are just going to have a quiet family staycation. He's over the moon that Lucinda is coming back as promised, was worried she'd just put him off. You know how it is with kids, out of sight, out of mind? Speaking of which, how's Jesse doing?" she asked, pouring herself another coffee.

"Really good, loves her new school, and spends every hour away from teaching duties on her art. I'm so proud of her, it's amazing how much she's changed."

"You know Lidia, I think it's amazing how all of us have changed these last two years. We faced fears, began new lives, for the better, I think. Except for Frank, whenever I think of him, I feel sad. How's he doing?"

Lidia sat up and inched her legs to the edge of the couch, "Okay, I guess. To be honest we don't actually know. He's so private, doesn't communicate with either of us, so we just give him his space."

"Oh? Well, Javi and I think it's really weird, how he suddenly leaves the priesthood, moves to England, then barely talks to any of us… Lidia, what really happened there? You must know something."

"What? No!"

"C'mon, you can tell me, after all, I've trusted you with my secrets, haven't I?

"This isn't the right time. There's sensitive feelings amongst all three of us. Nick doesn't even mention him, and I don't feel that it's my story alone to tell. But I'm sure he's alright, doing what he wants to do. I really feel that someday, he'll come back to us again, when he's ready. Believe me, okay?"

"If you say so," Becky said quietly, getting-up to put her cup in the dishwasher.

"And like you said, Beck, we've all turned a corner into the future, so let's not look back," Lidia said brightening.

"Right, heads-up, and like my momma said, 'even if the light's green, look both ways for traffic!'" Becky chuckled.

"And always carry Kleenex, an emergency tampon, and a quarter for the phone," Lidia added, giggling.

"Oh god, yes! I remember that," Becky rolled her

eyes. "Now, tell me, what's your *sposato* up to these days?"

"Nick? "He's all fired-up about a project uncovering the works of Renaissance women artists in Siena. He and Enza, she's an art restorer, have been thick as thieves ever since she introduced him to her new discovery."

"Really? Sounds interesting," Becky replied.

"It is. In fact, this weekend they're in Milan on an 'art hysterical quest' for what Nick believes is the Holy Grail of the Renaissance, an undiscovered master, or should I say mistress, of some very intriguing works." Then checking her watch, "Oh, it's almost time I pick-up Antonio."

"Okay then, I'll let you go…and Lidia, sorry I didn't seem supportive earlier. You'll do brilliantly, I love your blog."

"Thanks, Beck. Love to everyone there!"

"Ciao, kiss Nick and the baby boy for me."

"I will," Lidia said, feeling a little homesick.

ART HISTORY INTRIGUES

MILAN, THE CAPITAL city of the region of Lombardy, did not disappoint Nick; living up to its reputation amongst Italians as being too cosmopolitan, its architecture too modern, its pace too brisk, its people too uptight, to be truly 'Italian'; all of which made Nick homesick, as it was in these very respects Canadian, Torontonian to be specific.

A simple way to understand the different zeitgeists between Florence and Milan is this; the Milanese Prada fashions are boxy, in structured fabrics, their debut signature bag, a grey nylon no-nonsense satchel with a discreet grey Prada logo. While Florence's Gucci is all about sumptuous silks, soft as butter Merino wools, in colors as rich as the flowing fabrics. Their signature bag is caramel leather, covered in a pattern with a clever, interlocking 'G' motif. Despite their both being exclusive and expensive, the approach of the former is utility, the locus of the latter, luxury.

But the sumptuous food! That is definitely, 'no-holds-barred on the fat', luxurious. This is where the Milanese's inner 'bon vivant' betray them. From the fabulous, rich, flaky pastries to the luscious, creamy saffron risotto, and the richly breaded and butter-fried veal chops, even the pedestrian pizza is stuffed and deep-fried, crisp, heavenly, oozing with sauce and cheeses, as Nick discovered, upon taking his first bite.

He and Enza decided to treat themselves to a

pizza fritta each while waiting for the express train back to Florence, which would traverse through the main culinary towns of the Emilia Romagna region: Parma, home of the famous cheese and ham, Modena source of original balsamic vinegar, and finally Bologna, birthplace of the eponymous ragú Bolognese, and the country's indisputably best cooks. Their ultimate destination, Florence, would be reached in just over ninety minutes.

Nick reckoned the trip had been a success and expressed the same to Enza as they settled into their facing seats. Nick pulled down a retractable table between them, put his notebook up and began scrolling through the documents and images he'd recorded from the valuable, astute research Enza's colleague, Venera, had gathered. As he shared his screen with Enza, he stopped at an ancient letter, written by an abbot to his bishop, while visiting the convent of Sant'Ambrogio, a kind of report on the nuns' activities.

"Am I understanding this correctly Enza? It seems to me that he is concerned about the use and style of the devotional images some of the nuns are producing…he says the symbolism is obscure, at least to the Christian canon, and the attitudes of the figures appear too 'passionate', impious? Is that right, I'm afraid my Latin isn't what it used to be."

"Correct, and further, that he has rumors of perhaps a charismatic cell within this convent, called Il Cercolo Viola, the Violet Circle, who he thinks may be using magic rituals, but can't discover to what purpose."

"Hm, looks like our abbot is a spy for the cardinal."

"Yes, it looks that way. This may have to do with an earlier, medieval conspiracy from this convent to install a female pope."

"You're kidding!"

"No, this history has been suppressed, even to this day. But it's true, there is primary documentary evidence, anyway this episode might have made the church fathers suspicious of the nuns' activities, decades, even centuries later. Hence the abbot's annual visits."

"So, if there's so much suspicion and rumors around the convent's activities, why didn't the Vatican just shut them down?"

"Ha! That's where it gets really interesting, where the secular and the sacred intersect. Just look at the mention of high-born, noble women in the other documents as devout patrons of this convent, they go all the way up to the 'Warrior Woman' herself, Bianca Sforza, whose relative, Sister Manfreda, was part of the 'conspiracy'. They are the convent's protectors, this is their private world, their realm. Don't underestimate their matriarchal purview over such matters, and don't forget, that the pope himself, or at least a cardinal or two was usually a close relative."

"I see, I never thought about it like that. I'm going to start digging around to learn about this Violet Circle, I think it's the key to these strangely Expressionistic, kind of Proto-Gothic images."

"Oh, I think you're right. You have your work cut out for you though, Venera couldn't find anything, and she's like a dog with a bone where there's a mystery," Enza declared, leaning back in her seat, taking-in a deep breath, wishing she could have a cigarette and a nice cold glass of Lacrima Christi.

Just then came the welcome sound of the hospitality cart jiggling its way toward them, Nick offered to buy a bottle of prosecco, to celebrate.

"Salute!" Nick raised his glass, "Here's to a fruitful partnership."

Enza returned the salutation, took a long refreshing drink, then said thoughtfully, "It is intriguing how some of the ex-voto paintings Venera showed us in The Castello Sforzesco portrayed the Madonna, and even St Anne, holding a white iris, instead of the traditional, white Madonna Lily."

"I wondered about that too, I'm no botanist, so I

just thought it was a kind of local white flower, perhaps with a name like Maria Iris, or Queen Anne Iris…anyway, are you sure they're iris?"

"Oh yes, and I think they are indigenous, in Tuscany at least. Not sure about Lombardy, though. You could look that up, as a place to start."

"Good idea," Nick responded, scrolling back through some portraits, "but I guess the fact that in some of the images, the women wear purple smocks, or sleeves with interlocking purple circular floral motifs was just fashion?" Then turning the screen towards her, "Look here, Enza, this one of Bianca Sforza also shows her resting her folded hands on a red cushion with circles of purple leaves."

"Hm, well purple certainly was popular amongst aristocrats as it was the most expensive color to produce. But purple circles, could be a literal symbol for the Cercolo Viola. Perhaps she was patron? But, getting back to the ex-voto works…these were often created when a woman and her infant survived the rigors of childbirth."

"If the Violet Circle has something to do with that, then how?"

"Could be a medieval remedy for pain? As well as fervent prayer to the Virgin, by the expectant mother and the nuns of the convent she patronized."

"Were nuns also midwives? Could the expectant

mother even spend her confinement, along with her personal staff, in the convent?" Nick pondered.

"You know, it's possible, but I don't think there's any direct evidence for that." Enza shrugged. "Why?"

"Well, perhaps this Violet Circle were women who had delivered successfully using some kind of violet tincture, or tisane made and administered by nuns?"

"Yes, but where then, does the white iris come in?"

Nick sighed heavily and stroked his chin, "Don't know, except they're both flowers."

"Not quite enough, is it?"

"No, but I'm hoping research will reveal an answer. In the meantime, let's enjoy the passing scenery and drink-up before our prosecco gets flat."

Chapter Nine

WARMING-UP TO WINTER

WINTER, IN EUROPE, chestnuts are everywhere; the woodsy aroma from street-carts selling the hot-roasted nuts fills the air; the precious, jewelled marron glacé glisten in the pasticcerie windows; the bitter chestnut liqueurs enjoyed after dinner; in the bars, the nutty, fudgy Castagnaccio alla Toscana served with Marsala; and the mid-day snack of necci, a ricotta filled chestnut-flour crepe, hawked in all the markets, a recipe Lidia was working on for her blog.

Flavia introduced her to them at the Fierucola Market, she liked them, but thought she could do better, without adding more cooking time, so bought a half-pound of chestnut flour, a can of chestnut purée, took it home, and began to experiment.

Lidia felt pleased with the new dessert she'd created as she stood in the kitchen, hands on hips, regarding her vignette of *necci*, spread with Nutella, chopped chestnuts, sweetened ricotta, rolled-up, then dusted with icing sugar and piped zigzag on the top with purée.

Looks good, she congratulated herself, assessing the cake-stand artfully piled with the finished crepes. *Now just another element,* she took a few windfall chestnuts, bursting out of their spiky pods, looking like little porcupines, and scattered them on the orange paisley jacquard shawl she had draped casually over a corner of the beige marble ta-ble *…hmm…not there yet,* she grabbed a few roasted, unshelled nuts, tossing them here and there, knowing that a random 'arrangement' always looked best. Then just as she was setting-up her camera and tripod, she heard Nick's key in the door.

"Hi! We're home!" Nick shouted.

"Damn," Lidia mumbled under her breath as Antonio made a beeline for the kitchen. "Hi, little man. Did you have a nice time with papa in the park?"

"Uh! Uh!" Antonio stood on tiptoes, reaching for the carefully staged necci.

Lidia yelled, "No! No! Nick, can you take him please! I'm just getting ready to shoot!"

Nick swiftly scooped-up his son. "No touching mommy's work, okay?" Antonio's bottom lip began to curl. "Don't cry," Nick gave him a kiss, "I'll get you something to eat," he said, rubbing his little belly.

"Here, he can have these rejects, the first few never seem to turn out right," Lidia said, giving Nick a small plate of irregularly shaped, too thick, crepes.

"These don't look that bad. Anyway, I thought perfectionism wasn't your brand."

"I photographed those earlier, as the 'before' images, now I want to do these, to show what a little dexterity and patience can achieve. So please, both of you, get outta' here, before I lose my light!"

"Okay, we know when we're not wanted, eh Antonio? By the way, the 'afters' look great, good work," Nick said, as he took Antonio and his snack to the living room.

When Lidia got all the shots she wanted, she called them back to the kitchen, and put on some espresso. "Now, how would you guys like some of the real deal?"

"Antonio, say, 'grazie, mamma'," Nick coached.

"Gatzi, mamma," he responded, obediently.

"Bravo, Antonio!" Nick said, putting him in his chair.

"Bavo 'Tonio!" Antonio replied, smacking his hands together.

"Oh dear," Lidia exclaimed as she served the espresso and crepes. "I hope we haven't given him a speech impediment!"

Nick, pouring Antonio a glass of milk asked,

"Why would you think that?"

"I sometimes worry that immersing him in Italian, before he's had a chance to get English properly, has kind of confused him. I mean he doesn't seem able to pronounce his 'R's' at all. I hope he's not going to grow-up to be one of those soft 'R' speakers."

"Soft 'R' speakers? What're you talking about woman?"

"People who pronounce their 'R's' like 'W's'. You know…'wascally wabbit'?"

"Oh, you mean like Elmer Fudd?"

"Yeah, like Elmer Fudd. That can be a real social handicap, everywhere but England," Lidia asserted, cutting into a crepe.

"I know I'll regret asking, but why not in England?"

"Because that's how the 'Toff's' talk, the upper-class, they're wet-talkers too, spit a lot," Lidia shuddered.

"Well, guess we'll just have to move to England," Nick sighed ironically.

"Don't be absurd. If Antonio needs it, we'll just get him speech therapy, no need to emigrate," Lidia laughed, finishing cutting-up Antonio's crepe for him before he grabbed it. Then handing him the plate, said, "But being a soft 'R' speaker in Italy would be a real set-back. I mean when the Italians aren't elongating their vowels, they're hard rolling those 'R's!"

Nick looked-up from his crepes, "These, carrrra mia, are delicioso! RRRRinggrrrrazie!"

They both laughed at his exaggeration, and Antonio, looking from father to mother, joined-in, shouting, "Rrrr, rrr! Mamma!"

"Well, those are his 'R's'sorted. Guess you were just waiting for the right moment to say them, eh Antonio?" Nick smiled at his boy.

"Rrrr, rrrr!" he growled again at his father.

"Okay! That's enough!" Lidia said sharply. "Now he just sounds feral." She stuffed another piece of necci in Antonio's mouth.

Nick looked sheepish and shrugged, then deciding to change the subject, remarked, "I like how you've filled these, but ever think of layering them for a cake effect?"

"No, hadn't thought of that, what filling?"

"You could keep the chopped nuts and Nutella, but mix the puree in with it, and lose the ricotta, um…layer-in some roasted Hachiya persimmon pulp, drizzled with chestnut honey. Spatter with a dark chocolate sauce, and pipe-on some chestnut purée, decorate top with marron glacé and candied orange peel," Nick said, with satisfaction.

"Sounds delicious, but way too elaborate," Lidia said with misgivings, "my recipes keep it simple."

"It is simple. Just assembling really, with the exception of roasting a few persimmons and scooping them out, could be substituted with orange marmalade for the indolent," he said, licking a finger.

"Thanks, I'll mention it in the post, don't think I'll make it though."

"How many crepes d'ya have left?"

"About six, why?"

"I'll use them for lunch tomorrow, with creamed mushrooms, pancetta and Emmenthal, then we can finish the minestrone for dinner."

"What's for dinner tonight?" Lidia asked.

"Veal saltimbocca, capellini with pesto, simple salad."

"Good. I love your saltimbocca, the pan jus, nice and buttery, the veal perfectly pink…don't know how I *always* manage to overcook it."

"The trick is in 'The Hail Mary Flip'. The minute you lay the veal escallops in the hot butter, just recite slowly like this, 'Hail Mary full of grace, may the Lord be with you,' then flip them, recite again, transfer to warm plate, where they continue to cook just a little, finish your pan sauce and drizzle over them, voila! Perfectly pink saltimbocca. Pan should always be hot, escallops thin."

"Just recording that on my phone for next post, thanks Nick!"

"My pleasure as always, dearest Lidia. Now, if you and our lord and master here, will excuse me, I must dash, gotta' see a woman about a reliquary," Nick said, getting up to go.

SCENTS AND SENSIBILITY

WOW...THIS IS A nippy little number, Nick thought, being surprised when Enza picked him up in her red, Fiat 124 Abarth Spider convertible. He also recalled thinking, *can she drive this thing, like it should be driven? Bet she's a Sunday driver.* A chauvinist sentiment he was now regretting as his friend took the winding curves of the Tuscan countryside at a confident, if alarming speed. *She's enjoying this...I can see a little smirk curling-up at the corners of her mouth, those almond eyes sneaking a sideways peek at me. Must've read my mind. Well, I'm not giving her any satisfaction. I'm good. It's fine. We'll be there soon...I hope.*

Nevertheless, he found himself gulping hard and gripping the door handle even harder, as Enza rounded the last sharp switchback at the crest of the ridge. *Thank god it's all straight from here!* Nick let out a deep breath, as they roared along the snow-dusted allée of cypress leading up to the ancient abbey, now turned winery and hotel.

"You are in for a treat, Nick. This abbey, it goes back to the eleventh century, as a Dominican monastery and pilgrim hospice, as well as a robust agricultural concern, the Dominicans being very interested in oeniculture. In fact, it is said that this is the original home of Chianti."

"And where does the reliquary come in?"

"It was discovered in their nineteenth century deconsecrated chapel, used mainly for storage, but now the owners want to renovate it to create a reception-event space, to add to their hotel, restaurant, and cooking-school businesses. The Terrabuona estate is very popular in the Agritourism program, where visitors come to learn about wine, Italian cuisine and stay in beautiful, historic surroundings."

"So, why did they call you? Is this work done by a woman artist?"

"Don't know, haven't seen it yet. But today, I'm here on my family's business. My late husband and his brother owned a fine art and antiques studio in San Gimignano. After my husband died, I decided to keep my interest in it, until my brother-in-law retires. I do restorations, and consult on valuations and acquisitions," she said, coming to a crunching halt on the circular gravel drive.

A tall, big-boned, young woman with an aquiline profile and aristocratic bearing, greeted them at the door, introducing herself as Giuliana de' Medici, "And no, not that de' Medici, I'm afraid," she smiled with aplomb, anticipating what Nick gathered was a question often asked of her.

She led the pair through the niche-lined entrance displaying antique statuary, to the tastefully appointed reception area, a space supported by expansive arches, walls hung with Gobelin tapestries on ornate brass rods depicting genre scenes of medieval rural life. All capped by a high ceiling, terminating in an oculus, around which swirled a trompe l'oeil, celestial motif of pale, blue sky, puffy clouds, and delightfully chubby putti. The four-foot-tall reliquary stood on a large, circular marble table beneath the oculus.

"Please Enza, feel free to open and inspect it as you see fit," she invited her, with a smile. "We haven't touched it since it was removed from a cupboard in the sacristy." Then turning to Nick, "Can I offer you a glass of vin Santo?"

"That would be lovely, thank-you," Nick responded, his mouth feeling quite dry from the ordeal of his journey.

"And you, Enza?"

"Yes, your vin Santo would be perfect," Enza replied inspecting the bas relief carvings of two patrons, knelt in prayer, facing each other on either side of the doors. "Hmm, too bad the paint and gilt are so faded. Look's like there's some worm damage too," she muttered, passing her hand over the Gothic-arch frame and the tell-tale pinholes of infestation. She carefully pulled-up the pin securing the panel-lock.

Nick stepped-in to help, opening-out one panel, as Enza unfolded the other, to reveal a splendid triptych of Saint Catherine of Siena, receiving the stigmata from the risen Christ, as on one side, the Virgin Mary, flanked by Saint Gabriel on the opposite panel, witness in adoration, each holding a stem of white flowers.

"That is glorious, the colours are still so vivid," Giuliana said, as she set down her tray and passed a glass to each of her guests.

The trio stood thoughtfully admiring the work, quietly sipping their drinks when Nick, peering closely at the side panels, declared, "Either those are badly painted lilies, or those two are holding iris."

"What? Let me see." Enza moved-in front of him,

pulling her reading glasses down from her forehead. "Ah! Well-spotted! The brushwork is quite thick there, perhaps a clumsy attempt at restoration, but yes, you can see they're iris."

"Does that matter?" Giuliana asked.

"It does to us, and perhaps to the value of the work itself…" Enza trailed-off, sliding-out a carved panel beneath the central image, "Aha, here it is, the relic," she exclaimed, holding-up an ebony and silver crucifix, in the centre of which was a crystal, encasing a slim lock of blonde hair. "A lock of Saint Catherine of Siena's hair."

"How do you know it's Saint Catherine?" Giuliana asked.

"First, there is the scene of receiving the stigmata of Christ, which St. Catherine did, second, she wears the black habit of the Dominicans; Catherine was a mantellate, a group of pious women, self-administrating, informally devoted to Dominican spirituality. Third, at her feet are scrolls and writing implements, she was a prolific writer and influential theologian, her magnus opus being *The Dialogue of Divine Providence.*

"Catherine became quite influential with Pope Gregory XI, persuading him to move his court from Avignon to Rome. And, unusually for a woman, acted as his papal nuncio, a kind of ambassador. As a mystic, received the stigmata from Christ, and became his celestial bride.

"After canonization in 1461, a cult of worship grew-up around her amongst the Tuscan female nobility. Ultimately, Catherine became the patron saint of Italy. I admire her immensely, as a young girl was intrigued by her story, even took her name for my confirmation."

"What are her life dates, Enza?" Nick asked.

"Born 1347, died 1380, in Rome, where she was buried."

"Died in 1380, but not canonized until 1461, so I guess you can date this work to at least 1461 onwards," Nick pointed out.

"Yes, probably, but it could be earlier, as she was revered and renowned particularly in her home region. If we were to date it stylistically, because of its strong Gothic features, expressionistic quality, and emotive sensibility, it may belong to the fourteenth, not the mid to late fifteenth century."

"But what about the relic? Wouldn't her relics have been acquired from the church by the devout, later, after canonization?" Giuliana added.

"Not necessarily, if it even is an authentic relic!" Enza interjected.

"Right, if all the relics of the 'true cross' were brought together, you could build Noah's Arc," Nick added laughing, inspecting the crucifix, while Enza investigated further into the niche behind the sliding panel.

"And, what else do we have here," she said, pulling out a purple leather pouch. Opening it carefully, she removed a small cut-glass vial, at the bottom of which was a thick, dark brown substance. Easing off the ornate, gold-capped cork stopper attached to a long gold chain, she took a whiff. "Oh, that's a little musty, but still a strong scent."

She passed it to Giuliana, who took a sniff, wrinkled her nose and offered it to Nick, who inhaled deeply, and proclaimed, "Not wholly unpleasant, after all this time, strong, and yes, as you say, Enza, 'musty'. Wonder what that scent is though, I can't identify it."

"Not sure either," Enza replied, as Giuliana shrugged in accord. "Well, whatever it is will have to wait. If you'll excuse me, Giuliana, I need to take some notes and a few pictures, then we'll be on our way. I can send a report in two weeks, when we'll talk further."

"Sounds good. I'll leave you in peace, just call me when you want to leave, I'll be in the next room," she said, gathering-up the glasses, making her way out.

ON THE WAY back to Florence, Nick and Enza spoke at length about the function of reliquaries, and the clergy's trade in dubious relics, Enza postulating that the crucifix and the vial may have been plague amulets, used to ward off the disease that hit Tuscany particularly hard in 1450, killing nearly half the population.

As they approached the city gates, Nick asked pointedly, "So, tell me, what do you really think about the date of that reliquary?"

"My first impression was that it fit the period when I assume our La Maestra's bottega was active, circa 1440 to1470. And stylistically, being an anomaly for that time, if my dating is correct, points strongly to it being from her studio, if not by her hand."

"Why didn't you say that, then?"

"Because I'm not sure, I never pronounce definitively based-on first impression. I need to research thoroughly, perhaps consult another historian, then report to the owner. There's no point in saying something that gets hopes-up you might need to retract later," she replied, turning into the city. "Where can I drop you? Home?"

"No, I need to do a little Christmas shopping for Lidia's gift. Smelling that vial reminded me that she's out of her favourite scent. Do you know of a good perfumery here?"

"Oh yes, an exceptionally good one, in our area, near Santa Maria Novella, it's the oldest perfumery in Europe, founded in the sixteenth century. It's housed in a former monastery, the monks then being herbalists and chemists, who really created aroma therapy. Look, it's just over there. Since the light's red, I'll drop you here."

"Thanks Enza, talk soon," Nick said, clambering awkwardly out of the low-slung sports car.

Entering the pristine, light-filled 'temple of perfume' Nick could see the echoes of its monastic past, the cross-ribbed vaulting, the rose windows, the bands of stucco quatrefoil outlining the corner spandrels, all evoking the aura of a once-sacred space. His eyes roamed along the gleaming counters and display cases holding rows of glistening, glass bottles filled with precious, jewel-coloured scents. Nick chuckled quietly at the irony of a business devoted to sensuality, seduction and luxury conducted in a place once dedicated to asceticism.

"May I help you, sir?" a classic, blonde beauty greeted him.

"Yes, thanks. I'm looking for a perfume for my

wife, something special for Christmas."

"What does she currently wear?"

"White Bergamot, that's always been her scent, but I'm open to other options," Nick smiled broadly at the woman, not minding if he spent a while sampling and perusing.

She led him to a display counter, and set out four sample fragrances, spraying the first on a strip of absorbent paper, offering it to him to inhale. As he did so, she explained, "This one has a base of bergamot, with overtones of orange, and hints of sandalwood and patchouli."

Nick wrinkled his nose, unsure of whether he liked it, "Don't think it's really her, a little too exotic, perhaps."

"I see, then we're looking for something more floral?"

"Yes, I think so."

"How about this, bergamot base with rose, lily of the valley and a hint of pear."

Nick sniffed the sample thoughtfully, "Getting closer."

"Then, try this one, it's a new formula for us, a twist on a classic," she misted a new strip, from a pale-purple bottle.

The minute the scent hit the air, Nick's olfactory sense was aroused, he took the strip and breathed-in deeply, his eyes popped wide open, "That's it! That's the scent!"

The woman looked pleased, "Yes, it is distinctive, isn't it?"

"No, I don't mean… it's very pleasing, but it's a scent I've been trying to identify and research. What's in it?"

"The base is iris Florentina, orange blossom and a hint of lotus, with bergamot, of course."

"What color is this iris Florentina, in nature, I mean?"

"White, but its essential oil gives off a fragrance very like violet, in fact in the middle ages and renaissance, the root, called orris root, was dried and ground-up to burn as an inhalant, which has hallucinogenic properties and smells strongly of violet when used in this way.

"It was used ritually by religious mystics, and as a pain relief. The white iris was also the ancient symbol of Florence, until the thirteenth century, when we broke with the papacy, then it became a red iris."

"Really? And how long have you been making this scent?"

"The original formula came down to us from the fifteenth century, from the monks' manuscripts, they're in a book that is part of our archives. I think it is called a 'grimoire'. But as I said earlier, this particular scent is a new formulation for us. Our perfume with a base scent of white iris has gone through countless iterations. If you are really interested, you could contact our director, he will be able to tell you more," she offered.

"No, that's fine for now. I'll take a four-ounce bottle of the second scent, the bergamot rose cologne, and do you have this iris Florentina in a small eau-de-cologne?"

"Of course, would you like them gift-wrapped?" she said. "Also, can I show you our lovely all-natural scented soaps, they are hand made and hand packaged."

Nick chose a pretty box of four floral soaps for Voula's Christmas gift, relieving Lidia of one more Christmas burden.

Lidia and Antonio were out when Nick got home, so he quickly stashed his packages and headed for the study to email Enza about his exciting discovery. Then, sitting back, contemplating the implications of his finding, he was seized by a bold determination. Logging onto his university's website, Nick printed-off the application for sabbatical leave and set about writing his submission.

Chapter Ten

FROSTY THE SNOWMAN

ANTONIO WOKE-UP TO a rare sight in Florence; it was as if the city had been turned upside-down in a giant snow globe. All night it had snowed and snowed, quietly, stealthily, transforming everything with its frigid touch. The little boy pursed his lips as he contemplated this miracle, deciding it must be explored, embraced. He threw off his blanket, jumping up and down in his cot. He began to shout, raising his arm, pointing out the window to the courtyard.

"Hey! Hey! Little man, what's all this shouting about, eh?" Nick asked, lifting his excited son from his cot. "Yes, that's snow! It snowed last night while we were asleep. Let's get you changed and fed, then we go out and play in the snow, okay?" Antonio nodded vigorously in agreement.

After he'd finished the business of pasting the last drop of porridge in his hair, Antonio squirmed to be let down so he could open the next door on his

'Frosty the Snowman' advent calendar, hung on the kitchen wall. Lidia picked him up, to get his treat from that day's window. "Uh-oh, Antonio, looks like somebody's been pushing the season. Apparently, there's only one week left until Christmas…Nick!"

"What? So, I had a chocolate. Alright, I'll buy some and put them back."

"It's not the same, it's supposed to be a count-down," Lidia said, as Antonio opened a random door, and struggled with unwrapping his treat.

"Good luck with that, he can't count. Not reliably well past four, anyway."

"Doesn't matter, it's the spirit of the thing," she sighed, unwrapping the chocolate for her child. "Here, Antonio, better eat it quick before your papa does. And look! Today we can go outside and make a snowman just like Frosty."

"Fosty," Antonio shouted, drooling chocolate spittle down his chin.

FAME AND FORTUNE

TO MAKE THEIR snowman, the Pontis decided to go to their favorite park, the Giardino di Carraia, behind the Palazzo Pitti. The Park was a popular retreat for urbanites wanting to roam several hectares of natural woodland beauty, kick around a soccer ball, snooze on a bench, or let their children loose in the playground. They were not alone in their quest for the perfect deep patch of pristine snow with which to make their sculpture, in fact, the park was a busy hive of visitors, eager to play, and create in the snow.

"Over here, Lidia! Here's the best spot," Nick yelled to her, carrying Antonio on his shoulders. He stopped at a drift against a copse of evergreens. "There now, little man. Let's get to business," Nick directed, letting him down. He scooped-up a handful of snow, judging its 'packability', shaping it into a large ball, then rolled it over and over as it got bigger. Antonio helped him roll until it was just the right size, Lidia taking pictures of their progress.

Next, they all pitched-in making a ball half the size of the base, to become Frosty's belly. Then Antonio, now getting the hang of it, was given the task of making the head, with final shaping by Lidia. Nick picked-up his boy, who held the head, having the honor of placing it on the belly, giving life to the legendary cartoon character.

Then, Nick twisted-off a couple of twigs from the base of an evergreen for the arms. Lidia got a bag of props out of her purse, Nick guided Antonio in placing the carrot nose, chestnut eyes, and raisin mouth. Then of course, what snowman is complete without four dried apricot buttons on his waistcoat?

Satisfied, they took several selfies with Frosty for posterity, then Antonio, regarding the little figure, asked, "Where's his hat?"

"Lidia?" Nick looked at his wife.

"Uh-oh! Damn, sorry little man, I forgot to bring one."

Antonio looked down, lips trembling and started to sob, "Fosty's not live, no hat."

Lidia looked forlorn at Nick, who took-off his toque, and placed it on Frosty's head at a jaunty angle, "Now, look! Antonio, he's alive, with his hat on now, okay?"

Antonio looked-up, "Not top hat! He's not live!" he shouted hitting the top of his head.

Nick searched for a quick answer, "Yes, he is. He's a Canadian snowman because we're Canadian right? And we wear toques, see mamma has a toque, you do, and now Frosty does too!" *But I gave mine to that stupid snowman, now my ears are freezing,* he thought, smiling bravely.

Antonio stopped sobbing but seemed unconvinced until Lidia distracted him, suggesting, "I know what'll be fun, lets play a snowball game. You and papa against me, lets see who can knock Frosty's hat off the most times, okay?"

The idea of throwing things, knocking things down, as well as beating his mother, held great appeal for Antonio, who quickly forgot all about the top hat, and enthusiastically joined his father making a stockpile of snowballs.

After several salvos, most of which were won by Lidia, Nick, bending down to make more ammunition declared, "This is great, isn't it, cara?"

Lidia, carefully crafting another missile, responded, "Yes! It's lovely, the park's so much less crowded than ours at home, no off-leash charging, pooping dogs either. The streets safer, pedestrian friendly, restaurants kid-friendly too."

"Makes you want to stay here for longer. I'd love for us to experience the spring here, what the countryside and the city's like in bloom," Nick said, raising his voice, optimistically.

"I know, before this, we've only been here in the humid, tourist summer," she responded, lobbing a snowball at Frosty's newly placed hat, missing it intentionally to keep the play going.

"So, let's stay longer! Our visas are for a whole year. You're happy here, right? And Antonio's adjusted well …so, waddya say?" Nick said, trying to act nonchalant, as if the idea had just occurred to him. He picked-up Antonio to throw the next ball, which landed at Frosty's feet.

Lidia picked-up another ball and shot it at Frosty's nose, knocking it sideways, "Are you nuts? You have to go back after spring break…you can't just go awol!"

"I know that," Nick said, tossing a snowball from hand to hand, "but, I could apply for a sabbatical," he said, heaving it straight at Frosty's toque, knocking it off.

"Yay, pada we won her!" Antonio shouted, picking-up the hat, reaching, stretching, until his father lifted him up to replace it. "No Antonio, we *beat* her."

Antonio shouted again, raising his arms over his head, "We beat her, pada!"

"A sabbatical!" Lidia marched over to Nick, "for what, and for how long?"

"To do research for six months, on the mystical group of Il Cercolo Viola, and the works of La Maestra of Milano, then publish," Nick replied, dropping his last snowball.

Antonio, quietly sucking on his wet mitten, looked in anticipation from one parent to the other.

"Well, this is news! We need to talk more about this, Nick," Lidia said, her strained voice betraying the reasonable calm she wished.

"Yes, we do," Nick said, swiping the toque from

Frosty's head, stuffing it into his pocket. Hoisting Antonio onto his shoulders he announced, "But we're going to La Beppa for some pizza first."

LA BEPPA WAS too noisy, and Antonio too excited for Lidia and Nick to continue their discussion, so back at home, with their snoozing son snuggled between them on the couch and the fire roaring, Nick laid-out his plan.

"What I want to do on this sabbatical is to delve deeper into female religious and artistic culture, for now there's a picture emerging of a charismatic group of nuns, patrons, and artists, perhaps centered on Saint Catherine of Siena. But I don't want to explain their devotion and practices in terms of a cult, which would be exploitive. Instead, I see it as a kind of private, hermetic space women carved-out to express their spiritual, creative selves, and the truth of their inner lives."

Lidia was gently stroking her son's hair, listening quietly, surprised by the depth of insight, and feeling Nick had for these women, long dead, and forgotten. "I see. Obviously, you really care about this, I haven't seen you enthused about a project for ages that wasn't about cooking. You know, one of the reasons

I suggested our time-out here was because you were becoming cynical about teaching, maybe heading for burn out."

"I didn't realize it then, but I was becoming the stereotypical 'grumpy old professor', sleep-walking toward retirement. But now I've woken and can see where I'm meant to go. This discovery has just changed everything, or it will, if I can get that sabbatical."

"How do you think your application will be received by the new dean?"

"I think he'll support it to the committee, he's under pressure to have a curriculum that is more inclusive and diverse. A real challenge as Italian Medieval and Renaissance Art scholarship, done mainly by German men over a century ago, has buried any evidence of women's creative activities. So, there's a paucity of information out there, something AWA has done a good job in beginning to reveal."

"Why don't you work directly with them? They publish too, don't they?"

"Yes, but their patron set the goal of funding the restoration of seventy works, then it ends. And they're close to that now."

"Have you sent the application in yet?"

"No, I'm still working on it, but I've been in

touch with Ramsay, and she's all for it, which means a lot to have my head's backing, and the acting prof who took over my timetable is doing well and may welcome an extension to her contract. I still have to talk to the dean, although, like I said, I think he'll support it."

"What do you ultimately want to get out of this, Nick?"

"Ultimately, if I'm not jinxing myself, I'd say, becoming a professor emeritus, time and support for research. And eventually authorship beyond academic papers, to popular culture, maybe even tv or streaming content, and perhaps historical novels based-on the Violet Circle. There's a mystery at the heart of this story, which I'm beginning to solve, and it involves white iris and violets," he replied, eyes dancing with enthusiasm, his voice rising, as he gestured expansively.

"Really? How do flowers come into it?" asked Lidia.

"Well, as a symbolic motif, in the works I'm studying, the white iris has replaced the traditional Madonna Lily, because of its hallucinogenic, therefore mystic powers. And violet because the white iris root, when ground up, smells like violets. Did you know, the symbol of Florence is the white iris, well, red now, but research shows it as originally white, in fact this plant is so identified with the city that it's called, Iris Florentina. How's that for destiny!"

Lidia felt his emotions about to carry them both off into the land of popular authorship, and the doors it might open. "So, you're destined to be the next Dan Brown? And your 'La Maestra', the new feminist discovery as big as Artemisia Gentileschi or Hildegard von Bingen?"

"Are you mocking me? It's possible, that this will be my golden opportunity, Lidia. Anything's possible, if you set a goal and push hard for it, get the right connections," Nick replied, a little deflated.

"I'm not mocking you, but please keep your feet on the ground, otherwise this could get exploitive, not only of the subjects, but of Enza as well. Does she know your plan?"

"For the sabbatical, no, I wanted to talk to you first. As far as publishing, she would be credited too, and some of the net proceeds would go to further her work, which relies now on government grants and private patronage. She will always receive her due and could get on the lecture circuit, even outside of Italy, her English is certainly good enough."

"Well, it all seems exciting, but let's not see history just repeating, okay?" Lidia warned.

Chapter Eleven

THE LAST PINCH OF CORIANDER

"AAAHH," NICK GAVE out a loud yawn, as he stirred the filling for his tortellini.

"What's the matter with you?" Lidia asked, as she watched Antonio finally get the last spoonful of stew into his greedy mouth.

"Nothing, why?"

"You've been yawning all day. Didn't you get a good sleep?"

"No, not really, I had another 'Fellini' night."

"Oh? What do you mean a 'Fellini' night?"

"It's as if Federico Fellini was let loose in my subconscious and given a key to the attic of my memory, it's harrowing, exhausting too."

"Which of his films was it like?"

"Uh, this one I'd say, Amarcord, with a little Satyricon spliced-in."

"Yes, I can see that'd be exhausting, 'specially the Satyricon scenes," Lidia laughed, wiping the mess from Antonio's face, as he banged his spoon on the table.

"Does he want more stew? I can warm some up," Nick offered.

"Nah, he just wants to play, I'll let him run amok a bit before his bath," she said lifting Antonio out of his highchair, "Ooh, you're getting too heavy for mamma." Setting him on the floor, Lidia gave him an empty biscuit tin, "There, little man, lets see how long it takes to drive us crazy, okay?"

Antonio shouted, "Ma, ma!" and started hitting the tin with his spoon.

Nick handed her a glass of wine, "Thanks, I need this," Lidia said, sitting down to take a sip.

"Rats!" Nick tapped-out a spice tin labelled 'coriander', "Lidia, did you put this away practically empty, again!"

"If you know, why do you ask?" she shrugged nonchalantly. "Guess I was busy, just cleared the counter, forgot it needed to be refilled. Isn't there some unground in the spice cabinet?"

Nick reached around the cabinet, "Nope, not a seed. This is the last pinch; I need more for my filling."

"Can't you just use nutmeg or mace, like everyone else?"

"No, you know I don't like nutmeg, not even in eggnog, and mace, it tastes like sawdust,"

"Oh? And when, in this lifetime, have you tasted sawdust?"

"Every time I've eaten something flavored with mace, that's when. I'm going have to go get some more," Nick said, checking the time, "I can just catch Gus before he closes."

"Oh Nick, it's cold and raining, just stay and make do, please," Lidia sighed.

"It's only at the corner; I won't be long," he said, giving her a peck on the cheek.

"Take your umbrella, and don't hang around drinking grappa and gossiping, company's due in two hours."

"I know, I'll be back in five!" he shouted as he closed the door behind him.

"You'd better be, mister," Lidia mumbled to herself, checking a notice on her phone. It was Jesse, on FaceTime, "Hi Jess! How are you?"

"I'm good, just ordered your Christmas presents."

Antonio, hearing his sister's voice, shouted, and pointed to the phone, "Jess, Jess!" clambering on to his mother's lap.

"Shush now, little man. You can talk in a minute," Lidia said, as he rested his head on her breast and put his thumb in his mouth, then getting back to Jess, "You didn't have to get us anything, but thanks."

"It's just a few little treats and a toy for Antonio.

How's the potty training going?"

"Good, he's a very independent child, likes to put on his big-boy, pull-up pants, mostly backwards. He even thought it a good idea, one morning when we slept in a little, to change his pants himself! I faked still being asleep and let your dad take care of that one." They both laughed at the image.

"He's growing-up so fast, sometimes it makes me teary, specially when he gets frustrated trying to dress and throws his shoes across the room, insists on feeding himself, and won't hold my hand on the street…so stubborn!"

"Sounds just like nonno," Jesse said.

"Oh, you noticed," Lidia retorted. "I can't wait for him and Voula to come for Christmas, I actually miss the big lug."

"Me too, mom," Jesse said.

"And I really, really miss you! Please tell me you're not going to sulk all by your lonesome at Christmas…I hate the thought of you being alone, when we're all here celebrating. You should call Becky; they're having a quiet Christmas. Lucinda will be back."

"Uh-huh. I'll think about it. Anyway, Pickles and I are fine on our own, with a Cornish hen, box of Christmas cookies, and several bottles of prosecco."

"You're just afraid of running into Josh and Kate

at Becky's, aren't you? Haven't you made it up with them yet? Please tell me you're still friends."

"Yes," she answered peevishly, "just distant ones, at the moment. Where's dad? I wanted to congratulate him on the sabbatical. I'm so glad he got it," Jesse said, keen to change the subject.

"I'm glad he got it too, even if it means not seeing you for longer. But he's thrilled, we're having Enza, and another conservator, visiting from Milan, for dinner to celebrate. Right now, he's out on a mission to get some of his precious coriander seeds for the tortellini. Is that Pickles?" Lidia asked hearing a sharp, insistent bark."

"Yep, I have to go take him out. Ciao for now, mom. Ciao Antonio."

"Ciao, Jess," Antonio chimed in. Then Lidia, kissing the top of Antonio's head said, "Well, little man, I guess it's just you and me now…how about I give you a nice bubble bath?"

THE STORM BLEW ever more forcefully as Nick, having declined Gus' offer of grappa, quickly concluded his purchase, and left the shop. Lowering his head, tilting his big black umbrella into the maelstrom, he stepped-off the curb onto the slippery cobbles. Nick barely heard the gunned engine of the black Vespa bearing down, cutting close to the corner, sliding sideways, too fast, and too late for him to stop.

Suddenly, the storm exhausted its fury, the pelting rain subsided to a drizzle, the howling wind died to a whisper, when a siren's screech, cutting sharply into the newly peaceful night, startled Lidia, as she helped Antonio into his bath.

"Oh dear, little man, that's close by. Hope no one's hurt...bet it's that idiot, zooming around on his bloody Vespa. He's a menace! Nearly ran Flavia over last week. Yes, yes he nearly did!" Lidia laughed as her toddler shouted and splashed the bubbly water all over the tub.

"Well, I guess we'll hear about it when papa gets home, right? Speaking of which, where is he, eh?" she checked her watch, "He's been gone for close to an hour...I just know he's having grappa with that gossip, Gus."

About the Author

Loretta Gatto-White is a former food columnist, freelance journalist, and anthologist. Her essays, and poetry have appeared in literary anthologies, journals, and magazines. Her stories have been translated into Italian, published online and in print. The books comprising, *A Pinch of Coriander trilogy* are her first novels.

Website: www.gattowhitewrites.com

Available now in paperback and eBook:

A Pinch of Coriander
Trilogy
Book One: *Time Will tell*
Book Two: *The Truth About Secrets*
Book Three: *Long Way Home*

9 781775 034148